Three-times Golden Heart® Award finalist **Tina Beckett** learned to pack her suitcases almost before she learned to read. Born to a military family, she has lived in the United States, Puerto Rico, Portugal and Brazil. In addition to travelling, Tina loves to cuddle with her pug, Alex, spend time with her family, and hit the trails on her horse. Learn more about Tina from her website, or 'friend' her on Facebook.

Also by Tina Beckett

The Surgeon's Surprise Baby
A Family to Heal His Heart
A Christmas Kiss with Her Ex-Army Doc

London Hospital Midwives collection

Cinderella and the Surgeon
by Scarlet Wilson
Miracle Baby for the Midwife

Available now

And look out for the next two books

Reunited by Their Secret Daughter
by Emily Forbes
A Fling to Steal Her Heart
by Sue MacKay

Coming soon

Discover more at millsandboon.co.uk.

MIRACLE BABY FOR THE MIDWIFE

TINA BECKETT

MILLS & BOON

First published in Great Britain 2020
by Mills & Boon, an imprint of HarperCollins*Publishers*
1 London Bridge Street, London, SE1 9GF

Large Print edition 2020

ISBN: 978-0-263-08575-4

MIX
Paper from
responsible sources
FSC™ C007454

This book is produced from independently certified FSC™ paper to ensure responsible forest management. For more information visit www.harpercollins.co.uk/green.

Printed and bound in Great Britain
by CPI Group (UK) Ltd, Croydon, CR0 4YY

To my husband…as always

PROLOGUE

ADEM KEPLER REMEMBERED the car ride like it was yesterday. The rough blanket from his bed had rubbed his cheek raw as he tried to brace himself against the bumps on the dirt road he'd once called home.

His dad's breathless call had set the wheels in motion, the flashing lights of the plane that had sent them on a flight to a new country. A new home. He hadn't realized at the time just how sick his younger brother was until he was several years older.

But at fifteen, all he really knew was that his mother's tears seemed endless and his dad had a white pinched look around his mouth that said his family's whole world was about to change. Looking back, he could see it was a blessing in disguise and the flight into the night had saved Basir's life.

He'd had no idea of any of that at the time.

But he did now. Brain tumors knew no nationality. No financial status. No gender. All he remembered was the powerlessness and anger he'd felt as he left all of his friends behind.

The first years had been hard. Learning a new language. A new culture. But slowly, the angry teenager became a man who understood the sacrifice his parents had made, even though he'd hated it at the time. Where the seriousness of Basir's condition should have brought the family together, it had taken an already strained marriage and turned it into a battleground. They were too proud to seek outside help, so the arguments and fights had morphed into silence and resentment. His dad had lost himself in the restaurant he'd opened, spending more and more time away from the house.

Many of Adem's decisions had been the product of his childhood, even his decision to go into neurosurgery. And it was also why he'd petitioned the administrator of London's Queen Victoria Hospital to open a clinic in one of the city's poorest neighborhoods. When asked if he'd head up the project and run with it he'd jumped at the chance, becoming the clinic's director.

He could make a difference for people like Basir. He believed that. If he had anything to do with it, this new clinic would minister to those in crisis, whether it be illnesses, family relations or pregnancy. It was where his heart was. He might not have been able to fix his parents' problems—or the fallout from it in his own life—but maybe he could help others avoid some of those pitfalls.

If Adem could change one person's life for the better—just one—it would be worth it.

It had been his mantra as he settled into medical school, as he'd done his training and as he managed the clinic.

And he would allow nothing to come between him and that goal.

Ever.

CHAPTER ONE

Five years later

CARLY ELISTON WALKED through the halls of the NICU of the Queen Victoria Hospital holding a clothes hanger in one hand, while draping the bottom portion of a long slinky dress over the other arm. Navy blue with a scattering of sequins across the bodice, it had been an impulse buy—something for herself—after wearing three different bridesmaids' dresses. Four years later, that blue gown still had the tags on it when she'd loaned it to her friend. She'd told Esther she didn't need to return the dress, but her friend had insisted. It wasn't like Carly would need it any time soon. And evidently it had made a bigger hit than her friend had expected, since she and Harry Beaumont were in love and headed toward marriage.

Maybe the dress was enchanted. If so, Carly should wear it herself. She shook her head. No, she didn't need a man in her life right now. One failed relationship was more than enough. Fortunately her ex-fiancé had moved on to another hospital and a new love. Rumor had it that he was now happily married with a child of his own on the way. It was what he'd said he wanted most: a family…children.

For Carly, scarring and one lost ovary made the proposition of that ever happening iffy, although Kyle swore that wasn't the reason for the breakup. She'd gotten the old "It's not you, it's me" explanation. Maybe he just hadn't realized how hard it would be for her to get pregnant. They'd tried. For over a year. The harder things got, the more rigid and regimented her life became in an effort to somehow force her body to comply—to will that remaining ovary to function. And each time her period came, she became more desperate. Until Kyle finally…

Ugh! Old news, Carly. Get moving.

The feeling that she needed to shake her life up—to make a change—had never been so strong as it was right now.

When Carly leaned against the door and tried to juggle the dress so she could reach the latch, it suddenly swung outward, causing her to careen into someone on the other side.

A man.

Landing hard against his chest, she gave a quick glance up. Adem Kepler. Perfect. The doctor in charge of Victoria Clinic where she normally worked. Adem had kind of a playboy reputation—one which made her avoid him whenever she could. His relationships were "all fluff and no substance" according to reports. If there was anyone she wanted this dress to work its magic on, it was certainly not him. Despite the way her crazy pulse sped up whenever he was near.

And when he flashed that sardonic grin

at her—the one that had just now kicked up the left side of his mouth—she was a goner.

"Going somewhere?"

She planted her feet back under her and hefted herself off his chest in a hurry, trying not to be distracted by that smile or the slight accent that peppered his speech. After all, her American accent was still fairly noticeable, even after living in the UK for over ten years. "Sorry. I didn't expect the door… I was just trying to…" She took a deep breath to calm her nerves, which were spinning in circles. This was not quite the "change" she'd envisioned a few moments earlier. "I was taking this to my car before heading to work."

Adem fingered the fabric of her dress. "Nice. But this is not your normal style, is it? And the hospital fundraiser isn't until next year."

"Hospital…?" Oh, he thought *she* was borrowing this for a party. She swallowed, trying to push down her disappointment. There was no shame in borrowing a dress from someone; after all, she'd thought nothing of loaning it to Esther. It was more the fact that he assumed that wearing a dress like this would be out of character for her.

Wasn't it? At least for the Carly who'd been consumed with thoughts of babies during the last year of her engagement.

She'd bought the dress a week before Kyle announced his decision to leave, hoping to shake things up. Instead, the gown had hung in her closet, price tags still attached, until she'd loaned it to Esther.

Her face burned with embarrassment. "I know when the fundraiser is. And this dress is very much my style. I bought it, after all." She certainly didn't need to tell him why she'd purchased it, though.

Up went dark brows in…disbelief?

Oh, no, he didn't.

Her fiancé used to tease her about her lack of a social life too. Maybe that was another part of why he'd dumped her. If anything, she owed some of her seriousness to her mom, who'd raised her all by herself after Carly's dad died, working hard to make sure her daughter had everything she needed. It was something she didn't take for granted.

But that didn't mean Carly didn't know how to have fun. She tipped her chin up. Hadn't she said she wanted to shake things up? Well, maybe now was the time. She could start doing things differently.

"Just because *you* haven't been lucky enough to see me in the dress doesn't mean I haven't worn it."

You haven't, Carly.

"I never said you haven't worn it. But you're right in that I wasn't lucky enough to see you in it."

Oh, perfect. Now she'd come across as conceited. "Maybe some other time. Now if you'll excuse me..."

She waited for a moment, but he didn't move. He wasn't exactly blocking her path, but since the door behind her had already swung closed she would need to sidestep to make it around him.

"Do you have a few minutes? I was actually going to try to catch you at the clinic. I'd like to discuss some changes for the community midwife program we're putting into place."

Accent or no accent, she found herself bristling. "The women in that community need access to what we can—"

"Relax. I'm not taking anything away. I was here at the main hospital asking for additional funding for the program. It was approved. We're adding two mobile ultrasound machines. But we'll either need additional technicians or a few midwives at the clinic to be certified in their use."

Her heart stuttered in her chest. She'd put in a request last year for portable machines, but never dreamed…

She took a careful breath. Then another. Trying not to let her thoughts run away with her, although that was almost impossible with him standing so close. Looking so devastatingly handsome. She did her best to force back those thoughts. "I would like to be in on that training."

"I thought you might. So I hoped we might talk over tea. Does the request seem more attractive now?"

Yes. And it wasn't just the request that looked more attractive. How did he do that? No wonder he had a reputation.

"Okay. Can I meet you in the canteen after I take my dress to the car?"

"Of course. I'll see you there."

Five minutes later, her shaky hands free of everything except for her purse, she headed toward the canteen. She wished she felt a little more centered—a little more in control of her emotions. Crashing into him must have shaken her more than she realized, because as soon as he was out of sight, muscles that she hadn't realized were balled up tight went limp. So much so that she'd had to stop and lean against a wall for a few seconds to steady her legs.

But portable ultrasounds. He had no idea how much she'd wanted them—how much they would help everyone involved with the program. Or maybe he did, since he'd requested the funds.

They would no longer have to ask patients with issues to come into the clinic to have the imaging done. Some of her patients didn't trust government institutions, even hospitals, and were wary of such requests.

Reaching the canteen, she quickly spotted him at a table in the corner and took a deep breath, before giving him a cheerful wave and heading up to get some coffee. When she was stressed or nervous, her American roots came out, and she opted for that dark bitter brew her mom drank. Dumping a measure of powdered creamer into the coffee, she went to join Adem.

As soon as she dropped into the chair, he poured something from a little silver pot into a teacup. It was very black, almost thick looking. There were no tea bags anywhere. "Is that coffee?"

He glanced up. "Yes. Turkish style. I grind

the beans at home and normally brew it in my office. Today, I had to make do with an electric kettle. I see you're not drinking English tea either."

No, and she didn't really want to go into the reasons why. "I guess my heritage comes through sometimes too."

"Your mum teaches music at the International University?"

She hesitated and wasn't sure why. "Yes, she does. It's how I came to be in London years ago. When it came time to choose whether to continue my education here or in the States, I decided to stay near my mom."

"Same here. My parents moved to the central part of Hackney when I was in high school. My father owns a restaurant not too far from the clinic." Adem smiled. "I think he wanted me to take it over when I grew up. Luckily my brother showed a lot more promise in that area than I did."

"No sisters?"

"Nope, just me and my brother." His voice tightened slightly. "You?"

"Only child. Just me and my mom actually." She glanced at him. "My dad was an archaeologist, but he died while on a dig when I was ten."

"That must have been tough."

She smiled, her nerves finally beginning to settle a bit. "It was. But I have good memories of him." She'd been a tomboy growing up and had loved digging around in the garden pretending to find old bones and carefully cleaning them with a brush.

"You didn't want to become an archaeologist?"

"No. I thought about it, but my mom had complications during a pregnancy when I was young and lost the baby. She was never able to have another one. So, I guess it awoke an interest in prenatal health and delivery." That interest had become bittersweet as she wrestled with her own fertility issues.

"I'm sorry. About your mum, not your interest in babies."

Babies.

The way he'd said that word sent a shiver through her. She hadn't said she was interested in children. But he obviously hadn't meant it the way she'd taken it. There was no way he could know about her struggles. She decided to clarify, just in case.

"I'm interested in the moms *and* their babies."

He took a sip of his coffee, regarding her over the rim of the cup for a few seconds with those dark-lashed eyes of his. "That is what I meant, of course."

This time, the ripple of awareness had nothing to do with children and everything to do with the man himself. Oh, Lord, what was wrong with her?

"Of course." She decided to change the subject to something less sticky. "So we're getting portable ultrasounds. What's the certification process?"

"I looked into it when I put in the request. If I understood correctly, if you have a nursing degree—which you're listed as having—you'll need to do a year-long course. For midwives without that, it would probably take two years. Another option is to schedule the use of one of the machines in the field and request that a tech accompany you to the appointment."

That would work. "Will we have enough techs to go around?"

"That's where having extra staff would help."

"Frieda is a tech here at the hospital. We're friends. She might even donate an extra hour or two a week like some of us who already work at the clinic."

Adem set down his cup, hands resting on the table. His head tilted. "You're donating hours?"

Uh-oh. He didn't sound happy about that. "Is that a problem?"

"I'm just not sure why you would."

She was right. He wasn't thrilled. "The Queen Victoria uses volunteers for a wide range of services. Besides, I don't want to strain the funding more than necessary. After all, we may not have gotten those portable ultrasound machines if we demanded to be paid for every single second we're at the clinic. I know I'm entitled to be paid for rest breaks, but I like to donate hours where I can, just to help out."

"Understood, Carly."

The low gruff way he said her name made her insides quiver in a way that was too delicious for words. And that made her take a mental step back. Yes, he was a doctor, but he was also a man—and one she'd had trouble maintaining her cool around. She really didn't want to get into another problematic situation with a colleague, the way she had with Kyle. And actually Adem was practically her boss. It was okay to fantasize about the man. But it was absolutely *not* okay for him to know about those fantasies.

"Seriously, it's not a problem, right? I don't always have something planned every night, and it's not like I'm putting in a hundred hours a week."

She'd gotten some ribbing recently from a

couple of her friends who'd tried to get her to go out with them on a few double dates. But once burned… She really didn't want to jump into another relationship. And working extra hours gave her a ready excuse to turn down those offers.

I know you've been hurt, but there's such a thing as being too cautious. Wasn't that what Frieda had said?

But her relationship with Kyle had left a sour taste in her mouth. And if he really had left her because of her inability to have his baby… She didn't want to explain her issues to anyone else.

One side of his mouth kicked up again. "If we were talking about a hundred hours a week, that might be a problem. Since we're not, then no."

It took her a second to realize he was responding to her earlier comment. "I'm not. But I want to make a difference."

"Oh, you are. More than you know." There was a darkness to his gaze that hadn't been there at the beginning of their conversation.

She gulped down the last sip of her coffee, which was now tepid, and decided it was time to get out before her straying thoughts gave her away. "Speaking of differences, I'd better get myself over to the clinic and start my shift. Thanks for letting me know about the ultrasound machines. Any idea of their arrival time?"

"Not yet. But you'll be one of the first to know. In the meantime, I'll confirm the certification requirements and put them on the board in the staff lounge at the clinic."

"That would be great. Thanks." She nodded at the silver teapot and, before she could stop herself, added, "Someday I'd like to try Turkish coffee."

His eyes focused in on her. "Someday, Carly, I will make some for you."

And just like that, the reactions that had been percolating in the background were suddenly right there for all to see—nipples tightening, breathing growing almost frantic.

Do not get caught up in the man's charms.

"Thanks. See you later."

"I'm sure you will."

With a hard swallow, she forced herself to carry her cup and spoon up to the front of the canteen and deposit them on the conveyor belt. And then she pushed through the door and reentered the real world. A place where Adem was just an ordinary doctor and not someone who hit some of the buttons she'd done her best to deactivate. Evidently a few of them had decided to come back online of their own volition.

And that was the last thing she needed to happen with this particular man.

Today. Or any other day.

Adem sat back in his chair after Carly left the canteen and realized how little he knew about her. There was something reserved in her mannerism. Seeing her carrying that dress had surprised him, and he'd very nearly insulted her by blurting out the first thing that had come into his head.

The woman had a private life. At least she

said she did. One where she wore dresses like that for parties he knew nothing about.

He'd heard about a broken engagement, but never bothered much with gossip, so he didn't know the circumstances. Not that it was any of his business. It wasn't like he had a stellar track record in the relationship arena. He'd left that to his brother, who was now married and hoping for children of his own. It seemed that Adem's attempts to shield him from his parents' fights might have paid off.

The image of Carly in a slinky blue dress that he knew would play up that fair skin and red hair swam in his head. Damn.

It wasn't like the dress had just made him aware how attractive she was.

He'd already realized. And noticed. More than once. And was now wishing like hell that he hadn't.

Carly hung the dress next to the three bridesmaids' dresses. She was really glad it had worked for Esther. She and Harry made a great couple. And it wasn't like Carly was jonesing for a white dress with frothy layers. Not anymore. Thank God she'd never gotten around to actually purchasing her own during her engagement. She'd been too busy structuring her life around getting pregnant.

No, she was happy that some of her childhood and university friends were finding the love of their lives.

Did Kyle's exit from her life mean there was no one special for her? Her heart twinged, but nothing stronger than that, which was good after all that had happened. Maybe she'd been more in love with the idea of marriage and a family than in love with him, which in retrospect made her realize that marrying him would have probably been a huge mistake.

She had a full life. Maybe Carly was more like her mom—who'd worked hard to raise her after her father's untimely death—than she realized. Her mother had never remarried and seemed to find her fulfillment in her work. She was independent to a fault.

Like Carly? Probably. But it served her well now. She didn't need anyone else's company. At least not permanently. For the first time since the breakup, she realized she was free. Free to do what she wanted with her life, with no interference from anyone. Free to make her own choices about who to sleep with and when.

She glanced at the blue dress, once again seeing the surprise that had splashed across Adem's face when he'd realized it was hers. Oh, how she wished he really could see her in it.

Not going to happen, Carly.

She closed the door with a firm click. If all went well with Esther, it looked like Carly might be adding another dress to her collection before too long. And her other friends from university? The ones who still weren't attached?

She and Izzy Nicholson had met at the international school, along with Raphael

Dubois, who was one of the hospital's obstetricians, while she knew Esther McDonald and Chloe Larson from the midwife track at university. Life had sure given all of them some twists and turns. Chloe had a three-year-old daughter now. School had cemented their bond, and they'd all remained close over the years.

It made her glad of the decision to remain in the UK and build her life here.

Her mind swung back to Adem. They had at least two things in common. They were both in England because of their parents. And they'd both decided to stay here as adults.

So did lots of people. She'd worked at the clinic for a year now—ever since her breakup—and Adem had been there ever since Victoria Clinic opened five years ago. He'd done her interview, in fact.

Ha! That interview process had been kind of agonizing actually. His dark good looks had made it hard to think, even as he asked questions about her experience, her right foot doing a little dance as he'd detailed the job requirements. She'd had to uncross her legs to make it stop. At the time, she'd chalked it up to the stress of having her relationship implode in her face.

But it happened again. Several times, and when he followed her into her dreams one night, she decided maybe she'd better actively avoid him. Which had been almost impossible.

Well, she could no longer blame her reaction on her breakup, because at the meeting in the canteen, her foot had done its twitchy little best to keep pace with her heart. She'd uncrossed her legs again, planting both of her feet on the ground under the table. Her pulse hadn't been quite as easy to control.

And to find out he found her too dull—or unadventurous—to pull off a sexy dress…

Well, if the chance ever presented itself, maybe she would have to prove him wrong.

Lord! This was ridiculous. She needed to either get past this or figure out what to do about it. Doing nothing wasn't an option.

One thing her father had taught her at an early age was to pursue something until you figured it out. It was what she needed to do now.

But how was she supposed to do that when there were these weird itchy emotions popping to the surface one after the other?

She wasn't sure. But she'd controlled what she now called the Adem Twinges for the last year, so whatever was happening, she could just push those suckers back down until they got the hint and disappeared for good.

Her cell phone buzzed on her dresser, making her jump. She swallowed as she walked toward it.

It's not him. He has no reason to call you at home.

She picked it up, and then frowned. Naomi Silver, one of her patients. Naomi was almost nine months pregnant and so far had had a normal pregnancy—even if the events leading up to it hadn't been. Like Carly, Naomi had had her own fertility problems. She'd had adhesions that had kept her from getting pregnant for the last five years. She and her husband had even adopted a daughter, thinking they'd never have a biological one. And then, out of the blue, she'd gotten pregnant.

Her phone buzzed again. Naomi never called her at home, so her belly tightened.

She pressed talk. "Hello?"

There was no sound, except some kind of weird snuffling sound.

"Naomi? Are you okay?"

"I—I'm so scared."

Fear struck her heart. "What's going on? Where are you?"

"I'm home." A broken sob hit. "But my head hurts so much. I'm… Could I be having a stroke?"

Oh, God. A million possible diagnoses went through her head. Migraine. Preeclampsia. Eclampsia. Fetal demise. Her speech didn't sound slurred, but Carly wasn't willing to take any chances.

"Can you get to the hospital?"

"The clinic?"

She ran through the possibilities. The clinic could do C-sections in a pinch, but it wasn't set up with an MRI or other of the more expensive diagnostic equipment. "No. The Queen Victoria."

"Yes, I think so. My husband can bring me."

"Good. I'll meet you there."

The second she got off the phone, she tore out of her yoga pants and nightshirt and dragged on a black skirt and blouse, shoving her feet into low wedged heels that she normally wore when she was at the main hospital campus. Then she gritted her teeth and did the one thing she wasn't thrilled about doing. She called the man she'd just been trying to forget. It went to voice mail, but she left a quick message asking if there was any way he could meet her at the hospital.

And if he was with some woman?

She swallowed. Images she couldn't banish swept through her mind.

Dammit. Now was not the time.

She glanced at her watch. It was only seven o'clock. If he didn't get her message, there would either be a neurosurgeon present at the hospital or on call. She dialed the hospital number as she scooped up her car keys. Before she got an answer, her phone buzzed.

Adem.

She hung up on the hospital and answered his call. "Hey, I'm sorry to disturb you, but I have a patient coming into the Queen Victoria with some troubling symptoms."

"Like what?"

He didn't ask why she was calling him—a neurosurgeon for a pregnancy issue. For that she was grateful.

"She has a terrible headache, and she's really scared. And Naomi isn't one to panic without a good reason. Any chance you can ask someone to meet us there? I'm on my way in."

"I'm five minutes out. Headed back now. See you soon."

The line went dead. And if Naomi's problem turned out to be a simple migraine?

She grimaced. Simple migraine. That was an oxymoron if she ever heard one. It could be that a change in blood pressure had set one in motion. Except that many migraine sufferers experienced a lessening of symptoms during pregnancy due to the change in estrogen levels.

Well, she could hope that's all it was. And since Adem had volunteered to come without her specifically asking him to, it wasn't like he was changing plans just for her.

She hoped, anyway.

But he could have passed her off to a colleague, if that were the case.

It took her a little longer to make it to the hospital, since she had to come across town. By the time she arrived, Adem was in the A&E waiting area. He was in jeans and a white button-down shirt, the mixture between ultracasual and business attire a stunning combination that made her mouth go dry. She did her best to shake off her familiar reaction to him.

"Sorry to ask you to come."

"You didn't."

She frowned. "Sorry?"

"You didn't ask me to come, so don't apologize. It was my choice."

He was right. It was. But she still felt guilty. "I appreciate it."

"Were you on your way out?"

"Out?"

"You're dressed up."

She glanced down. Ah, she normally had a lab coat on over her blouse when she was working, and at the clinic she dressed a lot more casually, so maybe she did look different. "No. I tend to wear a skirt when I come in here, since the atmosphere is different from the clinic."

"I should have figured."

"What's that supposed to mean?"

Before he had a chance to respond, Carly spotted her patient walking up the path, one arm wrapped protectively around her belly, while her husband gripped her other hand, their daughter, Tessa, perched on his hip.

God. Naomi would be devastated if something happened to this baby. "That's her."

Grabbing a wheelchair, she rushed out the doors, not waiting for Adem. She had Naomi sitting in a flash.

"What's happening to her?"

Her husband Douglas's eyes were full of concern. Although they were from a deprived area of the city, they did their best to provide for their daughter and unborn baby. "I'm not sure, but—"

Adem went down on his haunches, a penlight in his hands. "I'm Mr. Kepler. I hear you have quite the headache."

"Yes. It's horrible. I called Douglas home from work. I never, ever do that."

Adem glanced up at the other man. "I'm glad you came. We'll get you inside in a minute. Can you follow the light?" He flicked on his penlight and took her through a set of commands right there outside of the hospital.

"Your pupils look good," he said. "Let's put you in an exam room. Douglas, you and…"

"Tessa."

Adem smiled. "You and Tessa can come in with her, if you'd like."

"Yes, please."

"Carly, can you get them in and registered? I'm going to check on something. I'll be right back."

Without another word, he walked back into the hospital. Had he found something troubling, despite his comment about her pupils?

Douglas wanted to wheel his wife inside, so Carly took Tessa in her arms, talking to the child as they made their way to the admissions desk. She went up to the window and explained the situation.

"Go on to exam room three. It's a slow night. We'll come in and get her information in a minute. I'll let Mr. Kepler know where to find you."

So Adem had stopped at the desk? There

was no sign of him right now. Maybe he really was canceling plans. He was dressed to go out to a restaurant. Her heart plummeted.

Well, so what? Hadn't he asked her why she was so dressed up?

None of your business, Carly.

Maybe not, but she was suddenly glad he thought that some man might want to take her out for a night on the town. She could have shown the neurosurgeon a thing or two, if it had been him. Especially after his reaction to her blue dress.

Really? Because you haven't shown a man a thing or two in, like...well...ever. Even her relationship with Kyle had been…sedate. Even as they tried for a baby.

Maybe Frieda was right. Maybe she really didn't know how to have fun.

Why the hell did she keep thinking about that?

She found the exam room and took Naomi and her husband inside. "Do you think you can get on the exam table? I want to listen to the baby's heart." Thankfully she'd remembered to wind her stethoscope and shove it into the pocket of her skirt before coming over.

Handing the baby back to her father and feeling a little twinge of emotion as he enfolded the child in his arms, she took out her stethoscope. "I'm just going to ease your slacks down."

Naomi was wearing the very type of stretchy wear that Carly had changed out of, so rolling down the waistband was a simple affair. A quick kick from the baby, visible through the skin of the woman's belly, assured her that it was alive. She breathed a word of thanks, warming the scope against her chest before placing it against Naomi's abdomen. She listened, moving the instrument to a couple of different spots before finding what she was looking for.

There. The baby's heart was strong. She counted the beats. Perfect. Not too fast. Not too slow. "I hear your baby." She stood and looked down at her patient. "Other than your headache, does anything else seem out of the ordinary? Any bleeding? Signs that your water has broken?"

"No. I was doing the dishes and a pain hit right at the back of my head. I had to grab the counter to keep from falling, it was that bad."

Adem came back into the room. "I've arranged for an MRI. They're just finishing up with another patient." He moved over to the bed. "Where is the pain exactly?"

She pointed an area just above the base of her skull.

Carly's gut tightened. Not a good place. It was near the brain stem, the part of the brain that controlled autonomic functions such as heart rate and respiration.

"And how long ago did the headache start?"

Naomi shrugged. "About two hours ago. I called Carly when it didn't go away."

He shot her a look she couldn't decipher. If he dared lecture her on giving out her phone number, she was going to give him a piece of her mind. It was what midwives did. Babies came on their own schedule. She'd delivered many in the middle of the night.

Yes, she could let another midwife go out on some of those calls, but Carly was fiercely protective of her patients and tried to follow them all the way through to delivery and beyond whenever possible. Yes, there were sometimes instances when she couldn't—for example if two women started laboring at the same time, but that didn't happen that often.

Naomi moaned and arched her neck. "It's back. It comes in waves."

Without him asking, Carly grabbed the cart that contained the blood pressure equipment, wrapped the cuff around the patient's upper arm and pumped it tight, waiting as the tick of the needle bottomed out. "One twenty over sixty."

"Within the normal range."

A nurse came in and asked Douglas to accompany her outside to get some information. Things between the clinic and the hospital were shared, so they should also be able to pull up Naomi's file with a few clicks of computer keys. Adem glanced at the husband. "If we're not here when you come back, it's because they've called us up for the MRI. The nurse can tell you how to find us, but one of us will try to catch you as we're leaving."

With that the pair were out of the room, leaving Adem and Carly to continue working to find the cause of their patient's headache.

Adem's phone buzzed. He glanced at it and then at her. "They're ready for us."

He was back to his businesslike self. Whatever she'd sensed in the canteen that day was gone. It had probably never been there in the first place. Just like that crazy dream she'd had. All just drummed up by her subconscious.

They helped Naomi back into the wheelchair. Fortunately her symptoms hadn't progressed to numbness or weakness. Just her massive headache, which was still worrying due to the location. Carly ran to tell Douglas and then met up with Adem and Naomi again at the elevator. As the doors opened, all Carly could do was hope for the best and pray that everything turned out well for both Naomi and her baby.

CHAPTER TWO

NAOMI WAS ON the sliding table of the MRI machine as Adem discussed what they were going to do. "We're actually going to do what's called an MRA or Magnetic Resonance Angiogram, which looks specifically at the blood vessels in your brain. We want to see if what you're feeling is caused by a problem with a vessel."

Her hands slid over her belly. "And if there is?"

"Let's cross that bridge if and when we come to it. Our on-call obstetrician is on her way in to check on you as well."

"I want Carly to deliver the baby."

Carly gripped her hand. "Let's take this one step at a time, okay? The most important thing is to keep you and your baby healthy. I don't want to jeopardize that in any way, and I know you don't either."

He appreciated her willingness to hand her patient off to someone else when necessary. She was definitely an asset to the clinic.

But damn, had his stomach knotted when he'd seen her name come up on his phone earlier. He'd been so shocked that he'd stared at it until his phone stopped ringing. He'd dialed her back immediately, though. Her voice had been breathless in a way that had made him think…

How wrong he'd been. He should have realized that the cool and calm midwife wouldn't call him for personal reasons.

And that was exactly why he needed to get his mind back on his job and off Carly.

Naomi's medical history included the fact that her mother had died of a brain bleed during the birth of her fifth child, and that fact alone warranted being very sure that there wasn't an aneurysm hiding somewhere in the young woman's gray matter.

There were sometimes genetic components at play.

"No, I don't want to do anything that would hurt him or her. Okay, let's go ahead. Are Douglas and Tessa here?"

"Yes, they're in the waiting room. This should only take about twenty minutes. You'll be back with them before you know it."

And if it was an aneurysm as he suspected? Then they'd have to decide whether to deliver the baby via C-section first and address the defect afterward. Or if they needed to treat the aneurysm first.

They'd already inserted the IV into Naomi's vein and they injected the contrast through a port in the tubing.

The tech then finished getting the machine set up, handing Naomi a set of earbuds that could pipe music through as well as allow communication between the tech and patient. "Are you feeling okay?"

"Yes. Just nervous about the procedure."

"That's perfectly normal. Are you claustrophobic? We'll need you to lie perfectly still for a period of time. You'll hear a lot of clicking and clacking from the machine, but that's normal as well."

"I'm not claustrophobic that I know of."

"Good. If you start feeling that way, the best thing to do is close your eyes. Blocking out your surroundings can help in a lot of cases. But if you start to panic, just let me know." He handed her a remote with a switch on it. "You can press this. And there are also speakers in the tube."

"Okay."

The tech helped her put the earpieces in and then they all went into the observation area. "I'm going to slide you inside the machine now, Naomi. Try to hold as still as you can."

The table moved forward until her head and shoulders were inside the tube. He pressed a button. "I'm going to start up the machine. I'll pipe some music in to help keep you occupied."

They'd asked her preferences in music and

found that she liked orchestral selections, so Carly had suggested the London Orchestra. Trevor, their technician, had scrolled through the selections until he found one.

Adem turned toward her. “You like the orchestra?”

“My mom plays cello for them. So yes, I’ve heard orchestral music almost my entire life. I’d better like it or my mom might disown me.”

He studied her for a moment, processing this new bit of information, before turning his attention back to the screen where images were flipping through at a rate that never ceased to amaze him. Carly sat next to him, crossing her knees, one foot wiggling back and forth as if having trouble sitting completely still. He seemed to remember her doing that nervous gesture a couple of other times. He touched her arm. “Hey. We’re going to figure this out.”

He wasn’t sure why he said it. Maybe because Carly was emotionally invested in her patient. It was a no-no, but was almost inevitable in certain cases. It was probably harder in the case of a midwife, who got to know her patients over the course of nine long months.

Interestingly enough, he'd known Carly for a year and felt like he knew very little about her still.

"I hope so. Naomi is the nicest person you'll ever meet. She had a very difficult childhood, but her family means the world to her. She told me that being a mom is her calling in life. She works as part of the cleaning staff at one of the larger hotels but is now on maternity leave for a few months." She paused, a shadow appearing in her eyes. "She had a hard time getting pregnant, so I'm sure this is especially scary."

"This is her first pregnancy?"

"Yes. Tessa is adopted."

"I see. I was surprised you came back to the hospital to meet her."

Her foot went still. "Naomi needed me."

So did a lot of people, judging from the

tired smudges around her eyes. “I wasn’t trying to lecture you.”

“I’m sorry, I guess I’m just worried. In the same way that Naomi’s family is her calling. She’s mine.” She paused. “Well, not Naomi specifically, but women like her. Those who have fertility issues.”

Fertility issues? Because of her mother’s problems?

The tech turned. “We’re getting close to the end. So far I haven’t seen… Wait a minute. What’s that?”

Adem got up and leaned over the screen, scanning it with trained eyes. *“Kahretsin.”*

The swear word rolled off his tongue before he realized it. But at least it was in his native language, not something either of the two people in the room would understand.

“What’s wrong?” Her voice came from behind him.

“She has an aneurysm. Posterior inferior cerebellar artery.”

“I’m guessing that means in the back of

the head. In the area she's having the pain. Is it bleeding?"

"Not yet. But it's large. If it does..." He didn't finish the sentence. Didn't need to. "I'm glad she didn't wait for it to go away. And she's actually very lucky she felt anything. A lot of aneurysms go undetected until something sets them off."

"Like childbirth." Carly came to stand beside him, her voice very soft. "This is exactly what happened to her mom. Only it wasn't caught. What happens now?"

"I want to examine the scans and consult with some of the other specialists, since there's a pregnancy involved. We'll have to put together a plan as a team. But I'll ask that she be admitted at least for the night so we can monitor her. You seemed okay with handing her off to an obstetrician."

"I am, absolutely. I'm only interested in her well-being." She glanced at him. "Adem, this might be the only baby she can have."

"We're talking about her life here. But

I understand what you're saying. Let me make a couple of phone calls while they take her to a room, and then I'll come talk to her."

He wanted the best outcome, for both Naomi and her baby, surely Carly knew that.

"I'd like to sit with her and her husband. I won't tell them any specifics, just that you're going over the scans and will be there shortly."

"That sounds good." He glanced at his watch. "Have you eaten yet?"

"No, but I'm okay."

His brows went up. "After putting in a full day at the clinic and then coming back this evening? Have you had anything since our coffee?"

When he'd promised to make her some. A huge mistake, because that thought had burrowed in his head, refusing to leave. What had started off as a polite comment had turned into something else entirely.

She tilted her head. "Have you had anything?"

It was a challenge. One he recognized and found himself responding to. Maybe it was the tiredness of a long day. But somehow he didn't think so. "Nope. Which is why I was hoping to grab something after we're done here."

The smile she turned on came out of nowhere. "Sorry. My mom is very independent. I'm a little too much like her. But I would like to know what the plan is for Naomi. Maybe we could talk about it there."

"That was my thought too. You choose where we go and I'll be down to see our patient as soon as possible."

The treatment plan was in place. Sitting in a restaurant that served Indian cuisine, Adem waited until they'd ordered before going over the results of his conference call. He'd spoken to Raphael Dubois, one of the hospital's obstetricians, and explained the situation. And while Naomi was far enough along to be able to deliver the baby, they both felt like to do so might cause the aneurysm to burst. So, ideally, it would be treated before she delivered. As soon as possible, in fact.

"I think we're going with an endovascular coil, which is less invasive than clipping the vessel would be."

"So no cutting open her skull?" Carly wasn't an expert on neurosurgery, but she knew a little. Clipping involved using a metal clamp to seal off the neck of the swollen blood vessel. But doing so meant having to do brain surgery, whereas the coiling procedure sent a catheter up through the femoral artery until the defect was reached. A thin metal coil was then released into the aneurysm, cutting off its blood supply, just like clamping would do. For Naomi, she could see exactly why they favored the one procedure over the other.

"No, no cutting."

The waiter served their food with a flourish that made her smile. If only she could be more like that. Maybe it really was time to clear away some of the cobwebs that taken up residence in her life. When the server left, she said, "He seems to be enjoying himself."

"Yes. I find that enjoying oneself sometimes means immersing yourself in the moment. In the unexpected."

He said it with a grin that sent her pulse spinning out of control. Frieda's words came back to her: *There's such a thing as being too cautious.*

Was that how others saw her? As cautious? Unable to immerse herself in the moment or to do something unexpected?

Maybe in her race to get pregnant, she really had lost sight of what made life fun. But she was not about to admit that to this man. "I know how to enjoy myself as much as the next guy. Or girl."

One brow went up, and he leaned back in his chair, crossing his arms over his chest. He didn't believe her. The man knew how to rattle her chain, that was for sure, and from the twitch of his lips, he looked like he knew it too.

Maybe it was time to do something unexpected...so unexpected it would make Adem Kepler's eyes pop from his skull. So here was to immersing herself completely in the moment.

"Just because you haven't *seen* me in that blue dress doesn't mean I don't know how to wear it. I know how to have a good time. More than you can possibly imagine."

She used her sultriest tone on that last phrase. So much so that it made her cringe. And for a second, she was horrified when he had no reaction to her pained attempt at flirting. None. Zilch.

Then a muscle in his jaw popped once. Twice. "Excuse me?"

Now was the time for her to give a bark of laughter and say she'd been joking and that she didn't actually have fun. Not that kind of fun. But her pride wouldn't let her.

"You heard me."

"I heard you. I just don't believe it."

Hell, she was attracted to the man. Had been from the moment they'd met. She'd also said there was nothing she was going to do about it.

Well, why not? Why couldn't she do something? It wasn't like she wanted anything out of him. But he'd talked about immersing oneself in the moment. Why not this one? Adem was gorgeous. With just the right hint of danger. The likes of which she'd probably never meet again. What would happen if she pressed a little harder?

Doing so would risk a lot more than her pride, though. What if he rejected her outright?

Nothing could be as bad as being rejected by your fiancé. Or being unable to conceive a child. Right?

Maybe she could wipe away that heartache in one fell swoop.

Picking up her glass of wine with a hand that was much steadier than she expected, she took a drawn-out sip of the ruby liquid, then let the tip of her tongue touch the rim of her glass as if capturing a drop that had escaped.

Oh, Lord. What was she doing? Was she crazy?

His eyes tracked the movement and a wash of red marched up his neck. His gaze came back up and caught hers. Tangled for a long, long moment. “Carly…”

Here it was. The moment of truth. Just how brave was she?

Hell, he’d started this, hadn’t he? Acting like she couldn’t lose herself in the moment, even if she wanted to.

In a burst of courage she didn’t know she possessed, she set her glass down and leaned over her plate, her gaze spearing his. At least, she hoped it had. “I seem to remember someone promising to make me Turkish coffee.”

“Yes. I did. Do you have a time in mind?”

“How about now? I bet if I asked you to leave our food untouched and walk out of this restaurant with me, you wouldn’t.”

“Wouldn’t I?”

Acting as if he was either going to wait her out or call her bluff, he stayed put for several painful seconds before pulling out his wallet and throwing a couple of bills on the table. Then he stood with a suddenness that shocked her. Reached out his hand.

He really was. He was calling her bluff.

Their waiter immediately came over to the table. "I'm sorry. Is there a problem, sir?"

"I'm not sure." Adem slid a glance her way. "Is there? Or did you just not believe I would?"

Yep. He'd read her all too well. But she was about to show him how little he knew.

Her chin lifted.

Oh, Lord, she was really going through with it. With her heart pounding in her chest, she stood and placed her hand in his. "There's no problem at all. We've just realized we have somewhere to be."

Adem nodded at the money. "That should more than cover everything."

The man's eyes widened. "Yes...yes, thank you, sir."

Towing her behind him, he made his way through the thinning crowds toward the door. A surreal sense of anticipation began pulsing through her. The likes of which she didn't think she'd ever felt before. Even with Kyle.

Of course, she'd never played games like this. With her ex...or anyone, for that matter.

Even as she thought it, she wondered if things had been leading toward this ever since he'd promised her that coffee. No even before that. When he'd talked about ordering those portable ultrasound machines that she'd wanted so badly. She'd been so thrilled. So happy. Because he knew how much she needed them and it was so thoughtful of him to look out for her department like that. Was going with him a product of that? No, she was pretty sure it wasn't. More likely she'd been determined to show him that she could keep up with him just fine in the romance department.

Ha! Romance. No. This would be a single-use sexual encounter. Something she'd never done before. And would probably never do again.

They went through the door and he glanced back. "Were you hungry?"

Kind of late to be asking her that question, wasn't it? "I'm starved."

She tried her best to give the word a sensual subtext, but wondered if she'd failed miserably for a second, then he responded. "Good. Me too."

He didn't have to work at sounding sexy. That rough gravelly voice of his made everything he said sound like he'd just climbed out of bed after a long night of lovemaking.

She shivered. Would he sound like that after being with her too?

They made it to his car. "Do you want me to drive you to the hospital to pick up your vehicle?"

"Can we do that later? After…coffee?"

A sideways glance made her swallow. "As long as you're okay with it being much later. And the coffee may have to wait for another time."

Her teeth sank into her lower lip. "It wasn't really coffee I wanted."

"I was hoping that was the case."

She was probably setting him up for a huge disappointment. Carly wasn't the girl she was pretending to be. The one who knew all the right moves. But she was a quick learner, when she wanted to be.

And this was something she wanted to learn. With him. Even if she never got to use those skills again in her life.

Sex with Kyle had always been a little tame, even by her standards, even more so when all their thoughts were stuck on pregnancy. There'd been no spontaneity, no desperate need for each other.

Not like the need she felt right now.

He opened the door for her, and she slid into the passenger seat. As she reached around to fumble for the seat belt, he leaned over and kissed her.

And that kiss…

Mouth against mouth, hand buried in her hair, he hinted at things she'd only dreamed of. Her hand curled around the webbing of the seat belt, needing something to hold on to.

God! Tame was one thing this man could never be accused of.

Then he was gone, the door closing as he walked around to the other side of the car.

Somehow she managed to get the restraint buckled, although her hands were now shaking.

Once in the car, he turned to look at her. "Are you sure about this?"

Sure about what? The wisdom of sleeping with him? Or *wanting* to sleep with him? Those were two entirely different subjects. The latter was a resounding yes! The former? Well, she would examine that one later.

"Yes." He didn't kiss her again, but he did

drive with an intensity that spoke volumes. “Are we going to your place?”

“Yes. It’s close. About five minutes.”

She settled back in her seat, his hand on the gearshift doing funny things to her insides. Especially since his thumb was sliding back and forth along it in a way that made her mind conjure up sensations that were becoming very, very real.

Five minutes had never seemed so long. Or so short. Five minutes until her world changed forever.

Well, maybe not changed. But at least rocked on its axis a time or two.

She shook her head. No. She was making too big of a deal about this. This was sex. A man and a woman enjoying spending an hour together. Nothing earth-shattering.

Really? Then why was there a part of her that didn’t believe that?

Maybe because she hadn’t felt this shuddery awareness before.

She’d played it safe with Kyle. Every time. That cautious nature that had always seemed to raise its ugly head. That had gotten even worse with every failed attempt at getting pregnant. And their last few times together had definitely never felt…special.

This man had left his dinner behind for her. How was that for special?

She shivered. It wasn't like he'd had a fencing match with someone over her.

Unless you counted his empty stomach.

Adem pulled up in front of a block of flats just off the Thames that boasted curved facades and sweeping balconies. Her eyebrows went up. She was used to much simpler accommodations. After all, her mom's university work and orchestral involvement might have caused her classmates to ooh and ahh, but they were not high-paying careers. Not that any of that had mattered.

He pulled into an underground parking area and shut off the car. "Still okay? You've gone quiet over there."

Had she?

She glanced over at him, and the emotions that had started this whole process quickly rose back up. She would probably never spend another night like this in her life. And she found she very much wanted to experience the non-cautious side of life. At least this once. "Oh, yes. Still okay."

They made their way to the elevator, where he pushed the button for the fourth floor. Once the doors closed, he turned to her and tipped her face up, studying it for a second or two. His fingers brushed her temple and traveled down her jawline. "Hell, I want to kiss you. If I wasn't already giving my doorman a hint of what's about to happen, I'd show you exactly how much."

His doorman? Her eyes widened and tracked to a corner of the elevator, where a camera looked like it was pointed right at them. She gave a nervous laugh. "So no acting out a scene from a book?"

"That sounds intriguing." One brow went up, and he leaned forward to whisper against her ear. "I'll keep that in mind for later."

Oh, God. She had no idea what kind of

scene he had in mind, but several possibilities were streaming through her brain, reminding her that she might just be in over her head.

And she kind of liked it.

Playing it safe had always been her MO, so the fact that she was about to do something so outrageously out of character sent another little thrill through her. Her fingers went to his nape as she tugged his head a little lower, giving his earlobe a little nip. "I may hold you to that."

"I'm looking forward to holding *you* in my bed. And in about a thousand other places. Including my plate-glass window."

Her breath hissed in, causing him to chuckle and lift his head. "Don't worry, honey. No one will be able to see you except me."

She wasn't worried. But she was squirming, and certain parts of her were growing uncomfortably needy. "Unless the glass breaks and we tumble out."

"The glass is very, very thick. And very

strong." He cupped her face, eyes dark as he stared down at her. "We could do almost anything against it."

She swallowed. She'd meant her words as a joke. But his response sounded almost like a dare.

Well, if this was going to be a night for the history books, she was going to make sure the memory of it would last her for the rest of her life. "That sounds almost too good to be true."

His smile unleashed a barrage of butterflies in her stomach. "I'll have a few survey questions for you after the tour."

"Tour?" The word came out rough-edged, her need for him clearly evident, even to her own ears.

"Carly, didn't you know? I plan to take things one room at a time. One surface at a time. Until neither of us have a drop of strength left."

The doors to the lift opened with a suddenness that shocked her, and it took her a second to get her bearings. He put his arm around her waist and eased her into the foyer, where three doors faced them. Exactly how soundproof were these apartments?

She had a feeling they were about to test that feature.

Spinning her in his arms, he backed her toward the apartment on the right. "Not a single camera out here."

With her back pressed flat against the cool metal surface, his lips covered hers in a kiss that seared her senses. His hands slid behind her, curving over her bottom in a way that tilted her hips fully against him. She had no choice but to twine her arms around his neck and hold on tight.

A tiny portion of her brain hoped there weren't peepholes on the doors of the neighboring flats, but a bigger, less rational part didn't care. After all, she was soon going to be plastered against the glass in his apartment, right?

He pushed against her, leaving no question that he was as affected as she was. If he wasn't careful, they weren't going to make it inside before she came completely undone.

"You have no idea what you did to me back at the restaurant." His hand slid down the outside of her leg until he reached her knee, fingers curling around the back of it. "I could just do this…" He tightened his grip, causing the inside of her thigh to slide along his as her foot left the ground, skirt bunching up.

Was he actually going to do it right here? All he'd have to do was unzip. One tug of her garment would give him access.

Her eyes fluttered closed, not caring, just needing him so badly.

Then he was gone, her foot finding the ground again with a bump. "I need to be inside. Now." The growled words were at odds with the way he'd released her.

So if he needed to be "inside," then why had he…?

He pressed his forehead against hers as if reading her mind. "Inside my flat. So I can be inside of you."

The fact that he'd had to spell that out made her laugh. "Oh! I thought we were going to…"

"Yes. So did I."

He retrieved a key card and swiped it in a slot next to a locked mailbox. A latch softly clicked and the door swung open. They went through, and Adem kicked it shut with the back of his foot. Grabbing her hand, he led her through the living room, the black leather furniture standing out against the white wood floors. He must have a housekeeper. Somehow she couldn't see Adem dust-mopping under the sofa.

The image made her giggle.

The forward momentum on her arm stopped and went slack as he turned to face her once again. "You find something humorous about this?"

"No, I just…" She gulped. "No."

He turned her until she was looking at a huge picture window, out from which jutted one of those balconies she'd noticed earlier.

Suddenly she knew she wanted that.

Wanted all of it. Everything he was offering she was going to take. She might be sorry in the morning, but she would worry about that when it came.

Walking her forward, his lips touched the side of her neck, the warmth against her skin sending a shudder through her. It was all she could do to keep her eyes open so she could see where she was going.

And where she was going was to the end of the earth.

A remote part of her brain took in the view and stored it away for later, even as his hands swept aside her hair and continued to kiss her with light feathery touches, his body crowding hers from behind.

She glanced to the side, making sure there were no neighboring windows visible.

"No one can see," he murmured. "I promise."

How did he know that for sure? Had he tried this before?

No. Don't think about that kind of stuff. Just enjoy the moment.

He turned her in his arms and kissed her again, the same defense-shattering melding of mouths, even as she felt his fingers at the first button of her blouse. He slowly worked his way down, cool air rushing in to meet the heated trail his touch left behind.

Her blouse slid off, leaving her in her bra and skirt. His mouth left hers, his hands smoothing over her shoulders, moving down her arms, caressing the curve of her hips, and then he bunched her skirt in his hands, scooping up more and more of the fabric until his fingers touched the bare skin of her thighs. Then he found the upper edge of her lacy undergarment and tunneled beneath the elastic, taking a step back as he eased them all the way down her legs.

"Step out of them."

She did as he asked, and the bikini briefs joined her blouse on the floor. He surprised her by tugging the hem of her skirt back down.

"Are you ready, Carly?" He pulled his

wallet out of his slacks and took out a square packet.

She'd been ready ever since they'd left the restaurant. "Yes."

He turned her around to face the window once again. "Then welcome to the first stop on our tour."

Adem wanted her against that window so badly he could taste it. He'd intended on making it their last stop, but doctors never knew when they'd get "that" call. Besides, he really had had to reel himself back in as they stood at the front door. He'd wanted to just find home and take her. But unlike the window, someone could appear out of that elevator or one of the neighboring flats at any moment.

But when he was around her, he had trouble thinking clearly. Even when he'd first offered to make her that pot of coffee, his mind had been heading in this direction.

Her head fell back against his chest when he nipped the cords of her neck. Damn this woman was unlike anyone he'd ever known. So proper and cautious as she did her job. Uptight, even. And here she was squirming under his touch, willing to play a little exhibitionist game with him. He wasn't going to strip her naked, although hell if he wasn't tempted to see how far she was willing to go. And he'd bet she would stand there au natural if he asked her to.

He pressed his cheek tight to hers. *"Seni çok istiyorum... I want you so much."* The words poured out in his native Turkish, telling her each and every thing he wanted to do with her. *To* her.

Hands reached back, her fingers gripping his thighs, edging toward the hard strain of his erection, as she whispered, "Yes, yes, yes..." as if she was having just as much trouble waiting as he was.

It was now or never, and if her hands found what they were looking for, it would be later. Much later. Taking her wrists, he lifted them, flattening her fingers onto the pristine glass surface in front of them.

"Keep them there. You can use them later. On me." He smiled. "On yourself." Yes, he would like to see that. Very much.

Reaching around her rib cage, he found her lace-covered breast, the mound filling his hand as he pressed her to the glass. He caught the nipple between his fingers and gave soft rhythmic squeezes, the moan she gave going straight to his groin. God, he ached. It was all he could do to not to unzip and thrust into her. And he would. Soon enough. His legs splayed apart, trying to assuage the temptation by pressing against the softness of her ass, the slight friction almost driving him over the edge.

He backed off and found the hem of her skirt once again and pulled it up, baring her backside completely.

"Adem..."

His name in that husky accent drove him to unzip and release himself, allowing skin-to-skin contact for a few luscious seconds before tearing open that packet and sheathing himself. His hand skirted her hip, fingers dipping down and finding a moist warmth that made him reel. All that, and he'd barely touched her.

"*Tanri*, Carly."

Then again, she'd barely touched him and here he was fighting for control with every neuron he possessed. Still. He wanted to be sure.

Finding her, he did what he'd done on her breast, trapping her and stroking, squeezing, even as he gripped himself with his other hand and positioned himself. He remained there for several breath-stealing seconds. Then he thrust deep, burying himself and holding completely still. Except for those fingers, which continued to move while he luxuriated in the tightness encasing him.

As if she couldn't take it anymore, Carly pushed against his caressing hand, the movements transmitted to parts of his body that were already struggling. He upped the ante, using his thumb to slide along the small bit of flesh still trapped between his fingers. Her breath hissed in, her movements growing frantic.

The world outside of his window seemed to spiral down into one tight, sexy view: Carly pressed to that glass, squirming against it—against him—her breasts sliding with each movement.

Then with a sharp cry, she rocked his universe, pulsing against him, along him, into him.

It was all over. He drove into her again and again, the pleasure which had been padlocked inside him breaking down the door and pouring through him in a long stream he hoped would never end. He continued to rock to completion, whispering to her, telling her how glad he was that she was here. How he wanted to do more of the same, even as something inside of him began to wave a warning flag at the rush of emotion that was pouring through him.

He ignored it. For now.

Withdrawing, he turned her to face him,

and found her biting her lip. He leaned down and kissed it until she stopped. “Okay?”

She opened bright green eyes and regarded him. Then she smiled. “Mmm… can’t talk. Don’t want to talk. But very glad that glass held.”

A laugh bubbled up from somewhere deep inside of him, rolling out and clearing away whatever had been whispering at the edges of his consciousness. He folded her in her arms. “Me too. I have other things we can test for strength, though. Like the bed… The dining room table… The office chair…”

Her eyes widened, but she didn’t miss a beat. “I’m ready for the next stop on our tour.”

With that he swung her up in his arms and carried her into the bedroom.

CHAPTER THREE

HE WOKE UP to an empty bed. And some kind of note on the side table.

Glancing at the spot where the indent from her head still was, something shifted inside him when his hand reached for it. That same flare of emotion that had rolled through him last night. Instead of letting his fingers trace the pattern, he shook the pillow out and plumped it up until it looked like no one had even been here.

Those warning flags were waving again. Only this time they were flapping under hurricane-force winds, making him sit up and listen. Whatever this strange stirring was, it needed to stop. Now.

His parents had had a less than stellar marriage. Scratch that. Theirs had been that whole commitment-until-dead thing, even when it was so obvious that they were not in love with each other. His dad was a difficult man at times, though. He worked hard, but he didn't play hard. In fact, he rarely ever took any time for himself.

He'd spent much of his teenage years trying to shield his brother from some of what went on, afraid he'd blame himself since it was his illness that brought them to England in the first place. Adem had been angry at first as well, which had added another layer of guilt, although he'd been careful not to let Basir see it. Instead, he'd acted out in other ways, dabbling in things he'd had no business touching.

Fortunately that stage hadn't lasted long. And Basir seemed to be unaware of it—in fact, he seemed to be the only one in their family who'd been able to learn how to love. He'd even gone to work with his dad at the restaurant and was able to brush off his dad's foul-tempered moments.

Because of love, he'd said.

Love.

How on earth had his brother been able to find that emotion? Because he certainly hadn't had an example of it at home. Adem wouldn't know love—the romantic fairy-tale kind of love—if it bit him on the ass. And even if it did, he was almost certain he wanted nothing to do with it.

Hell! Prying himself out of the bed, he showered quickly before remembering the note. He assumed she wasn't simply in the kitchen making breakfast, since he had no sense of her presence.

Not that he would know what that felt like.

Or did he?

Walking into the bedroom clad in a towel, he picked up the paper.

Thanks for the tour. Didn't even realize you had a view of the London Eye until this morning. Headed back to the real world, though. Catching the tube to get my car.

That was it? She "didn't realize he had a view of the London Eye"? The Ferris wheel was one of the iconic landmarks of London. He guessed he should be glad that she hadn't been staring at it during…

Or maybe she had been.

A day that had started off rough suddenly felt worse. Much worse. Because he sure as hell hadn't been looking at anything but her. The whole night.

He swore.

Somehow what was supposed to be a light, fun frolic—since when had he ever used that word?—had turned into a road that was dark and curvy. And Adem loathed not being able to see what was around the next bend.

So he was going to take the kinks out of whatever this emotion was and set it back on a straight course. Kinks? He grimaced at the term. He'd discovered a few kinks he hadn't realized he had.

He sucked down a deep breath and blew it out, tightening the towel and wandering into the living room. His shift didn't start until nine, and it was barely seven in the morning.

He glanced at his phone and saw that

Basir had tried to call him about half an hour ago. Perfect. Maybe that's where some of his thoughts about the past had come from. Some subconscious tickle perhaps alerting him to be on guard?

Nonsense!

But still, he was going to wait and call him back later.

So what time had Carly left? They hadn't even gone to sleep until the early hours. If he were smart he would try to get another hour's worth of shut-eye before he headed to the clinic.

No. Wait. The hospital. He needed to see their aneurysm patient.

Their.

Kahretsin. He'd bet his last pound that Carly was already there, checking on her.

Feeling like a major slacker for even forgetting about the woman, he turned to head back into the bedroom, head tilting as something on the glass window caught his eye. Some kind of mark.

His jaw tightened as he walked closer and

realized exactly what those smudges were. Handprints. From their time in front of the window. Images floated around in his skull, bits and pieces of sight, sound and the sensations that went along with them. His body reacted instantly, despite all they'd done last night.

Yes, calling his brother and hearing all about his happy life would definitely have to wait until later. Until after he'd downed a few cups of coffee.

Coffee he'd never had a chance to make for Carly.

Grinding his teeth, he headed for the kitchen and grabbed a bottle of spray cleaner and a couple of paper towels. And in the same way he'd removed the imprint on that pillow, a couple of squirts erased those telltale marks. But not the memories.

He stood back and looked at the glass. There. You'd never know Carly had been here.

Then he saw the London Eye and remembered that note. As sure as the sun was quickly rising in the east, he knew that every time he saw that Ferris wheel, he was going to see her hands pressed against that glass.

He swore louder, letting the anger and frustration wash away whatever softer emotions were fermenting in his gut. Like the fact that he wanted to see her again. Soon.

But like she'd said, it was time to reenter the real world. Before he did something he might really regret.

Like fall for her?

Not going to happen. He was not Basir.

Unlike his brother, Adem had never fallen for anyone in his life. And there was no way a one-night stand was going to change that.

As long as he didn't let himself be put in a situation where it could—like sleeping with her again—there was no reason for that encounter to change anything.

Carly tried concentrating on what Esther was saying, even as she felt him enter the room.

That was ridiculous. You couldn't really feel someone come in.

She glanced back, hoping beyond hope she was right about it not being possible.

Nope. Not right. There stood Adem, looking freshly showered and dressed, while she was still in her clothes from last night—although she had jumped under the spray in the hospital gym to rid herself of his scent. She'd woken up in a panic of not knowing where she was, and that had changed to horror when she remembered what they'd done. She never let herself go like that. Never.

Not that there was anything wrong with it. There wasn't.

Except it had left a deeper imprint than she'd expected. Which was why she hadn't been able to get out of his flat fast enough this morning and had hoped beyond hope that she could get out of the hospital before he arrived. And she knew he would, since Naomi was officially assigned to a team of specialists which he was heading up. Carly had briefed her friend on the situation, and since Esther worked in neonatal intensive care, she'd brought her in to meet Naomi.

Esther's eyes widened slightly when she spotted Adem. Then she turned to Carly. "Have you got this?"

Got what? Adem?

Oh! She was talking about the situation, not her relationship. Not that there was one.

Her friend was trying to politely excuse herself. Did she sense something? "Yep. I know you need to get back to work."

Naomi smiled. "It was nice meeting you."

"You as well. Can't wait to see your little one." Then Esther murmured her goodbyes and slid from the room.

Adem moved in to stand next to her, and her pulse immediately started thrumming in her chest. She took a calming breath, hoping he couldn't see her reaction.

"Did something happen?" He glanced at the closed door, and Carly realized he was wondering why Esther had been in the room. His being here caused everything in her head to turn into a chaotic mess.

"No, everything's fine. Her vitals are still holding steady and the baby's heart rate is perfect."

"Good." He came over to the bedside, laying a hand on the edge of Naomi's mattress. "How's your head feeling?"

"Better. Maybe whatever you thought you saw on the scan turned out to be nothing?" The flash of hope in her voice tugged at Carly's heart. This was the hard part of her job. And no matter how much she lectured herself on not getting emotionally involved, she did. She loved her patients, many of whom had come to her for subsequent pregnancies, keeping her updated with pictures of their kids as they grew and changed.

Carly was the only one who seemed… well, static. Ever since she'd stopped trying to have a baby of her own, she felt stuck in place—her feet planted on an immobile sidewalk while conveyor belts of people whooshed past her into their own happy futures, some never to be seen again. Esther probably would as well. The world was leaving her behind.

Could that be part of the reason she'd jumped at the chance to sleep with Adem? To shake that feeling off? To prove to herself that she was still spinning on this globe called life, just like everyone else?

His voice brought those thoughts to a halt.

"I'll relook at everything, but I don't think there's been a mistake. I'll meet with the team this morning, and we'll come up with a consensus that keeps you and the baby as safe as possible. Okay? You've already met Esther McDonald."

"Yes. And everyone's been so nice." She reached up and gripped her husband's hand. "But I'm actually glad you came to see me. If for some reason you have to choose between me and the baby during surgery, I… I want our baby to come first, so—"

"Hey, stop." Douglas leaned down and kissed her forehead. "You heard him. He wants to keep you *both* safe."

The man glanced at Adem. "When will you make a decision about what to do?"

"Hopefully this morning. I've already called in Dr. Dubois, one of our obstetricians. And of course Carly will be there as well."

She would? She'd asked, but she'd known from the start that there were no guarantees one way or the other. "I want to be there. I have to be at the clinic this morning, though."

Adem turned toward her. "I actually called the clinic and asked them to do some shuffling, if you're okay with that." He smiled at the young couple. "Can I borrow Carly for a few minutes?"

"Oh, of course."

Her stomach dropped to the floor of her abdomen. What on earth could he want? Oh, God, hopefully he wasn't going to rehash last night or warn her that business and pleasure were to remain strictly separate. Not that she was ever going to sleep with him again.

Last night had been too…

Earth-shattering. There was no other word for it.

Plus there was that embarrassing little detail of her forgotten hairbrush. She'd left it on his bathroom counter, dragging it quickly through her hair before she exited the building. She hoped he'd just throw it in the trash bin rather than bring up anything about what had happened.

Feeling like she was trudging through some kind of thick sludge, she made her way to the door and went through it, letting it close behind her.

Adem looked neither happy nor unhappy, although she sensed a wariness in him that hadn't been there last night. Of course, she probably matched him in that department.

And that wasn't the only department in which they matched.

Oh Lord, Carly, knock it off! He says a few words in a different language and you're swooning at his feet.

No, she'd been swooning long before that.

But it stopped right here. Right now.

She jumped in first, not giving him a chance to say anything. "Look, if this is about the…um… London Eye incident—" Could she possibly think of a worse euphemism? "Then don't worry about it. I'm not expecting any more tours or anything else, so don't worry."

One corner of his mouth went up. "That wasn't what I wanted to talk to you about, but now that you've brought it up…" He went over to the nurses' station and picked up a handled paper bag. It was a lot bigger than what would be needed for a hairbrush. And it looked heavier.

"I'm not sure—"

"The restaurant knows me and opted to have our meals put into take-away boxes, which they sent to the apartment building. My doorman had them waiting in the refrigerator this morning. This is yours."

Her face turned to fire. Had the proprietors boxed uneaten meals for him in the past? And worse, they had to have known exactly why they'd skated out of there so fast. "How often do they have to do that for you?"

Adem frowned, the coming together of his brows erasing any trace of that sexy smile. "Never. They assumed one of us was ill."

She'd missed the mark by a mile on that one.

Her eyes closed. "Oh God, Adem, I'm sorry. It's just been a…" What could she say? A long night? A once in a lifetime event? An event that was never happening again?

"Hey, I understand. You also left something else, but I left the flat in such a hurry I forgot to bring it."

He left in a hurry? Why?

"Not a problem. I have extras at home. I don't need it back."

"How often does that happen?" he mimicked her words, but the frown had faded and the lightness was back in his voice.

She laughed. "Same as you. Never. So are we good?"

"If we can both put this behind us, then I would say yes."

Said as if he'd already done exactly that. It might be a little more difficult for her, but she was sure if she worked hard enough at it, she could forget about last night.

She hoped.

And if she couldn't?

Well, Adem's implication was that if she couldn't, then all would not be good between them. So she would have to make that happen. Somehow.

She took the bag from him and held it between them as if that would somehow magically jump-start the process of forgetting. "So when is the meeting this morning? And will the clinic be able to 'shuffle' things? I'm pretty sure I had two appointments, and if someone goes into labor, I'll have to go."

"If that happens, we can meet later and go over what the team decides. But ideally, you know Naomi better than anyone else on the team. I'm hoping you can let us know if we miss anything important."

"Thank you. I really want to be there for her until the end. And she wants me there. You heard her yesterday."

"Yes. And I want you to be in the operating room with us. I think she'll be reassured if she knows you're close by."

He wanted her there while he performed the surgery? She would have to digest that bit of information later. Her grip tightened on the handles of the bag between them.

Deciding to change the subject, she wiggled the sack. "Do I have time to go home and change?" She'd been planning to swing by her place on her way to the clinic. He might be fresh as a daisy, but even with her shower, she needed some clean clothes. And to do something with her hair.

"The meeting is at ten, so you have about two hours."

Plenty of time. "Okay, I'll be back, or will

let you know if there's a problem with one of my patients."

"See you at ten, then."

"Are you going back in there?" She nodded at the door behind her.

"Yes, I want to go over a few things and let her know what to expect, if we go ahead with surgery."

"Great, if you could tell her I'll see her later on today, I'd appreciate it."

"I will."

She waited for him to push through the door, giving him a quick wave as she took her bag and headed for the exit that would take her to where she'd parked her car.

She had two hours before the meeting. Two hours to change and somehow figure out a way to deal with him on a daily basis without feeling awkward.

And the best way she could do that was eat the food in this bag tonight, so it wouldn't be hanging around her house longer than necessary.

Once that happened, she hoped—*hoped!*—

that she and Adem would be able to move back to where they were before this all started. She would retreat like a turtle, going back to the safety of her cautious little life. And next time she was tempted by someone like Adem, hopefully she would be a little wiser about giving in.

Basir and his wife sat in his office. Adem wasn't exactly sure what this meeting was about, but his brother assured him it was important.

It must be for him to leave the restaurant. But something he couldn't tell him over the phone? And why was Adeline here?

His chest tightened as a thought hit him. Had the tumor come back? Adem hadn't asked about the periodic tests his brother had done.

"Is everything okay?"

Basir and Adeline glanced at each other, making the sense of foreboding grow.

Until she giggled. The unexpected sound made him blink, reminding him of the way

Carly had laughed in his apartment. But it also served to wash away that sense of impending doom.

"What's going on?" he asked.

Seeing his brother healthy and happy was good for his soul and made him feel he'd done the right thing in taking Basir under his wing all those years ago. Whatever irritation he'd felt the other day faded away.

He should be glad for him. Truly.

"We came to ask you something."

He frowned. "Okay."

"We're looking for a midwife," Basir said.

His heart seized for a minute before realizing they weren't talking about Carly.

"Sorry?"

Adeline spoke up. "A midwife. Someone you'd trust to deliver your niece or nephew, Adem."

A beat went by. Then two. Suddenly it dawned on him what they were getting at. "You two are…?"

Basir's resulting smile stretched from ear to ear. "Yes. We're going to have a baby."

Adem got up from his desk and came around to where his brother had also got up and caught him in a tight hug. “Congratulations.” He included Adeline in his smile. “Both of you.”

“Thank you. After three years, the time just seemed right, you know?” she said.

He didn’t know. Not at all. But for once, he wished he did.

Adem didn’t see himself having children any time soon. Or later. While he was happy for his brother, the only emotion that came up when he thought of children was dread. Maybe because in the midst of an unhappy home, he’d taken on so much responsibility at a young age. In some ways he felt like he’d already raised one child. And the weight of doing what was best for his brother had almost crushed him emotionally.

But he wouldn’t change it for the world, especially after seeing the obvious joy on Basir’s face. But doing it again?

He didn’t think so.

"What does Dad think?" He hoped his father would be happy for them, rather than weigh it in terms of how it would affect his business.

"I haven't told him yet, but I think he'll be happy. Even if he always did think you'd be the first one to give him a grandchild."

Shock rolled up his spine. Why on earth would his father think that? "I don't..."

"You're the oldest, Adem. It's that whole duty thing." His brother said the words as if the reasons were obvious. And maybe they were to Basir, or even his dad, but not to him.

"I'm nowhere near that point." He said the words with a smile he didn't feel. "But I'm happy for you."

"Thank you."

"So back to the midwife question?" Adeline's soft voice came through. "As you know, this is where we come for treatment. Or would we have to go to the Queen Victoria?"

Adem went back around his desk and

carefully sat down. Yes, back to the midwife question. "You would come here, of course. And all of the midwives here are..."

Basir shook his head. "We don't need all of them. Just one. Someone who makes you feel cared for and special."

Even though his brother was speaking in general terms and not referring to Adem personally, the same face kept flashing in his mind.

She didn't make him feel special. It hadn't been what he was looking for the other night. He'd needed sex, and she'd offered it.

His jaw tightened. It hadn't been like that at all, and he knew it. But to play it off as anything else was crazy.

And Carly was one of the best midwives at the clinic.

So did he send his brother to someone else to make it more comfortable for himself? Or did he tell Basir the truth? That he'd trust Carly with anyone. Look at Naomi. Someone else might have just told them to go to sleep and see if they felt better in the morning.

Not Carly. She'd met them at the hospital and had taken an interest in her patient every step of the way.

Still he hesitated before taking a deep breath. "Yes, there's a midwife at the clinic who is exceptional."

"What's her name?"

"Carly Eliston." He glanced at Adeline. "How far along are you?"

"Six weeks. We wanted to have it confirmed before saying anything to anyone. And we want to give it a few more weeks before we tell Dad."

Adeline was referring to his and Basir's father, since hers passed away just before their wedding three years ago.

"I can understand that. Let me talk to Carly and see what her schedule looks like. If she can take on another patient, I'll give you her number."

One of Carly's strengths might prove to be a thorn in Adem's side. She took such a personal interest in her patients that it was doubtful that Adem would be able to stand on the sidelines and out of the way.

But he would have to try.

"Is there a chance she'll say no?"

"I don't know. It depends on how many patients she has." Not to mention how she felt about taking on one of his family members. Maybe she wanted nothing to do with him and would say no.

As someone who'd protected his brother for years, that didn't sit well. But he'd have no choice but to accept whatever decision Carly made.

"We can understand that. Maybe if you could contact them in order of skill."

"I'll do that and let you know." Suddenly he wanted them out of his office so he could think.

"What was the name of the person you like the most?"

Hell. Why did he have to put it that way?

"Carly Eliston. And I don't like her the most. Just said that she gave excellent care."

Basir's head tilted and he looked at him funny. As if he'd heard something behind the words. Something Adem had almost certainly not meant.

At least, he hoped he didn't.

"That's what I meant."

Adem stood again, ready to end this impromptu meeting. "Congratulations again. I'll get in touch with Carly and let you know."

In reality he was supposed to see her today, when he did the coiling procedure on Naomi. He could talk to her then.

Or he could lie and ask someone else completely, saying that Carly was busy.

For his own peace of mind?

He already knew he wouldn't do that. When it came to peace of mind, his was normally the one sacrificed for the good of his brother. And he couldn't bring himself to regret it.

Even if the next nine months turned out to the longest he'd ever endured.

* * *

Naomi was getting her surgery. Thankfully she'd continued to do well, but since her blood pressure had crept up a bit, the decision had been made to go with Adem's suggestion and place a coil in the bulging vein and cut off its blood supply.

Dressed in surgical gear and paper booties, Carly was already in the surgical suite when Adem swept into the room, hands held up so that a nurse could snap gloves on his freshly scrubbed hands. "Is everyone here?"

He glanced her way with an inscrutable expression, but didn't address her. Something in her chest twinged.

Did he regret asking her to be in the room? She'd held Naomi's hand as they'd administered the anesthesia drugs, the woman's eyes struggling to remain focused on hers, a slight flare of panic appearing before her lids flickered and finally closed. It made her throat clog. Even though Carly had never faced anything like this, she could imagine the things that might fill her mind as she was wheeled into the room: Would she ever see her husband again…would her baby be okay…would she be normal?

Just before Adem had come in, Carly had leaned over the sleeping woman and said, "I'm right here, Naomi. I'm not leaving, no matter what."

And if Adem asked her to?

Why would he? They'd seen each other in passing at the clinic over the last couple of days, but other than being there when the surgical team met, he hadn't gone out of his way to speak to her. If anything, it seemed almost like he was avoiding her.

Or maybe it was that she was avoiding him.

Which she was.

Raphael Dubois was on call at the hospital, if they needed him. And the neonatal ward was ready as well, Esther having told Carly to call her at the first sign of trouble—even before the call officially went to the NICU. They were as prepared as they possibly could be.

Adem moved to the table and gave the go-ahead for the contrast dye and imaging to start. He then made a small incision in Naomi's femoral artery and proceeded to feed the catheter through the opening. The process seemed to take forever as he stared at the screen where the aneurysm was now in sharp focus, a rounded bowl that looked like some kind of strange fruit that was attached to the tree by a stem.

"Preparing to enter the location. I'll need the microcatheter in a moment."

From what she'd understood from the meeting, he would thread another smaller catheter up through the one he was using now. It contained a thin platinum coil that would fill the aneurysm and cause the blood to clot, effectively cutting off its blood supply and preventing it from rupturing.

"Okay, I'm in place."

The surgical nurse next to him passed him the instrument, and Adem fed it through in the same way he'd done with the original catheter. The process was painstaking and seemed to take forever, even though Carly had been told to expect a couple of hours of standing. The standing wasn't the problem. It was that with each ticking second, there was the possibility that something could go terribly wrong.

No different than any birth she'd assisted.

That wasn't exactly true. This was dealing with a part of the body that was much harder to fix if a mistake was made.

And yet while there were lines of concentration clearly visible on his face, Adem's hands were remarkably steady and his breathing even and regular. Just like always.

How did she know what his breathing normally looked like?

She closed her eyes for a second to stop that image from forming.

She knew what it looked like. Intimately.

And right now, Adem gave off a vibe of confidence. She could remember times when she'd been worried about a patient's welfare and had had to mask those emotions, wall them off from both the patients and herself—so that she could do her job. Without that ability, she might as well throw in the towel and quit.

It was probably the same with Adem.

"Here we go, people."

She assumed that meant that he was getting ready to put the coils in place. With a flick of his thumb, a hair-thin fiber appeared on the screen and began making a series of what looked like loop-the-loops that quickly filled the defect.

"Giving the electrical charge…now."

The electricity caused the coiling material to separate from the catheter, allowing it to remain in place once the instruments were retracted.

He surprised her by not pulling out immediately after that happened, but remained in place, staring at the screen with narrowed eyes.

Kind of like he'd stared at her, when he

strained within her, staying exactly where he was for what seemed like a long, long time.

Oh, God. She put her hand to her throat. Where had that come from?

Very grateful to the mask that shielded most of her face, she swallowed several times, struggling to coil her emotions and shove them back in their container. But unlike the endovascular procedure Adem had almost completed, they weren't cooperating nearly as well.

A couple more deep breaths, though, and she was back in control. And as she glanced at the screen, she saw that the aneurysm seemed less "bright," although she wasn't sure if that was the right word.

Adem must have thought so as well, because he said, "I'm happy with the placement and how it looks. Getting ready to move out."

The process of withdrawing the catheters was a whole lot quicker than the time it had taken to position them. But that made sense, since he'd had to find the perfect path that would take him to the heart of the problem.

And her perfect path? The one that would take her to the heart of the problem with Adem?

Well, she was still trying to find it.

"Placing the closure device."

He must have seen her head tilt, because a few minutes after pressing what looked like a plunger in the area on Naomi's leg, he glanced at her. "I'm closing the incision I made in the artery with a collagen plug. It's faster than manual compression and allows her to become ambulatory more quickly. It dissolves in a few weeks."

Okay, that was interesting.

"Thanks for the explanation."

A nurse assisted in clearing away the tubing from the procedure and Adem nodded at the anesthesiologist. "Let's wake her up."

"Okay. Reversing now."

While a couple of the nurses continued to organize the room, Adem watched Naomi's face. When her eyes flicked open, Carly saw him take a deep breath. Maybe he hadn't been quite as unruffled as he'd seemed. That was good, because she just now realized how tight her own muscles had been.

She'd always thought Adem was a skilled surgeon, but watching him perform that surgery had made her heart swell with admiration. Maybe because Naomi was her patient and she was glad of the outcome. But she had a feeling it was more than that.

The anesthesiologist came around and murmured to the patient and then removed the endotracheal tube. "How are you feeling?"

Naomi's eyes tracked to his face. "Did it work? Baby?"

The croaked words made Carly's chest tighten. She wasn't concerned about her comfort or even attempting to answer the question. Even though she probably wouldn't remember these next moments due to the amnesic effect of the medication, her first semiconscious thoughts were for her child.

Adem put his hand on her shoulder. "It worked perfectly, and your baby is fine. We're going to wheel you back to recovery in a minute and let you get some rest. I'll let Douglas know how things went, and he can come see you in just a little bit."

Naomi looked past him and found her. A slight smile appeared, and she nodded.

Maybe Naomi would remember, after all.

She was so glad she'd stayed. So glad she hadn't let her personal feelings over what had happened with Adem deflect her from doing what she thought was right. And being here with Naomi had been the right thing to do. One of those cases when, like her patient, she put her own comfort to the side and worried about someone other than herself. "I'll go wait with her until her husband is allowed in."

"Are you sure?"

"Yes. I'll head over to the clinic afterward."

"Okay. I have one more surgery here, and then I'll be over as well." He smiled. "And I left your missing item on your cubicle desk. And later, I need to talk to you when you have a minute."

Her missing item. The hairbrush.

She wasn't sure why he'd felt the need to tell her that, or why her heart had picked up the pace when he said he needed to speak to her. She was just going to ignore her reaction, though, and keep on ignoring it until it became second nature and that crazy night of Glass Panels, the London Eye and her Lost Hairbrush faded into the past. After all, there was nothing she could do to change it. Any of it. And she wasn't sure she would if she could.

So why not just enjoy the memory for what it was: a thrilling night that, in the end, changed nothing.

CHAPTER FOUR

"MY BROTHER IS expecting a baby and needs a midwife."

Carly wasn't sure what words she expected to hear, but those were not them.

She'd gone from elation after Naomi's surgery, to fear that he wanted to rehash what was already over and done with: that night at his flat.

Blinking, she tried to catch up with reality. "Your brother?"

"Yes. I should have said he and his wife haven't been assigned a midwife yet. They're expecting their first child."

"The brother who's working with your dad?"

Adem gave a slight smile. "That's right. He's the only brother I have."

"Oh...yes. I should have remembered

that." Being around him again was bringing all those feelings from the other night back to the forefront. Not good. Not good at all. Hadn't she vowed she was going to keep things professional from now on? "You want me to take them on as part of my patient load?"

"I do. They're already patients of the clinic. If you have space, that is."

Suspicion crowded her thoughts. Was it odd that right after she'd spent the night with him, he suddenly wanted her to be his sister-in-law's midwife?

"May I ask why?"

He frowned, leaning against the white wall of the clinic foyer. "Do I need a reason?" His head tilted as if realizing something. "Ah. You think the other night might have had something to do with it. I can assure you it didn't. If anything, it made me think carefully about whether or not to recommend you to them."

And that thought horrified her even more. Had that night been that awful? "I don't really understand what that has to do with anything."

"I don't want to make things any more awkward than they already are. For either of us."

Okay, he had her there, because things had been awkward. For her at least, and a little part of her was glad that it was for him as well. That he hadn't been able just to brush it aside as if it had never happened. "Okay, that's understandable."

"If you don't want to do it, I'll understand."

Since she'd just said she didn't know what that night had to do with anything, she'd be a hypocrite if she suddenly didn't want to have his brother and his wife as patients. "You might, but I wouldn't. Of course I will. I'd like to meet them, if I could. Sooner rather than later. You know I like to follow my patients for as much of the pregnancy as possible."

"I know. Which is why I told them about you."

He had? A warmth infused her that had nothing to do with Adem's future niece or nephew. "I'm flattered."

"Believe me, it has nothing to do with flattery. I just know they'll get excellent care."

"Because of Naomi?"

"Not just her. I've watched you with your patients. While I personally think you might get a little too emotionally involved with them, I also know that it means that nothing will get by you."

"Thank you. I think."

He laughed. "It was a compliment."

She couldn't hold back an answering smile. "I wasn't quite sure."

"I'll have them call you to set up an appointment, if that's okay, in the next couple of days."

"That would be perfect. I look forward to meeting them."

He pushed away from the wall. "Thanks for doing this. I do appreciate it."

"Not a problem."

At least, she hoped it wouldn't be one.

Less than an hour later, her cell phone went off.

"Ms. Eliston? My name is Basir Kepler. My brother heads up the clinic."

She knew exactly who he was. She was just surprised that his brother was calling her so quickly, and that Adem had given them her cell phone number. Maybe he wanted to let her talk to them first before making any firm decisions.

His voice sounded very much like Adem's, with those low gravely tones, but he sounded younger somehow.

Or maybe he was just less cynical.

Did she really think Adem was cynical? Maybe. One thing she did know was that he was very good at keeping his emotions in check. Except for that night in his apartment.

Only that hadn't been emotion. More like lust. Or worse, just biological need.

Except he'd been so sexy. So…focused.

She cleared her throat. "Adem was just

talking to me about you." Too late she realized she probably should have used his title rather than talking about him so informally. Hopefully she didn't give Basir any wrong ideas.

Wrong ideas? Like what? She'd slept with the man, for heaven's sake. She sure wasn't calling him Mr. Kepler during that. But she also didn't want Adem's brother to think they had a relationship. Because they didn't. It was one night. And that was all it was ever going to be. She would make sure of it.

To cover up and hopefully divert any personal questions, she asked about him and his wife. "Tell me a little bit more about yourselves and your hopes for the baby?"

"Adeline is on the line with me, so I'll let her do most of the talking."

Soon thoughts of Adem were abandoned—at least on a temporary basis—as they discussed what they knew so far about the pregnancy. It was their first baby, and they wanted to try a home birth, if possible.

The usual excitement grew as it always

did when she spoke with a new patient. Maybe she lived vicariously through her patients, allowing their joy of discovery to become her own joy. Or it could be Adeline's bubbly enthusiasm, or maybe just how happy they both sounded. And that's where the difference came in. She sensed a genuine contentment in Basir that seemed to be missing from Adem somehow. Or maybe that was her imagination.

Fifteen minutes later, she'd posted a memo to herself on her phone. She was going to meet Basir and his wife here at the clinic in her cubicle. Later she would go to their home and go through what they needed to have in place for the birth.

"It was nice talking to you, and I look forward to meeting you both."

"Thank you," Adeline said. "Adem speaks very highly of you."

He did? That still left her dumbstruck… that Adem would have wanted her to be personally involved in the case. It also gave her a tiny thrill that warred with the lecture she'd given herself about not getting emotionally involved with him. If that were even possible.

It was. She would make sure of it.

"Well, I'm glad I can help. I'll see you next week."

They said their goodbyes and Carly continued on her way, glancing back as if Adem might have suddenly materialized out of thin air. Thank God he hadn't.

It didn't matter. Because like it or not, Adem was going to be involved in this pregnancy and birth and so would officially be a part of her life. At least until this baby was born and Carly was off the case.

Carly was going to be Adeline's midwife. She'd stopped by yesterday to let him know that they'd met and agreed on the hows and whys. And what had been a lazy current of uneasiness over suggesting her had turned into stiff gusts that were getting stronger by the day. Maybe it didn't have as much to do with Carly as it did with his brother himself.

Of course he deserved to be happy. Adem had bent over backward to make sure that had happened after Basir's surgery and treatment. But could it be that having the evidence of that happiness staring him in the face reminded him of how different he and Basir were?

Not that Adem wanted marriage and babies. And he especially didn't want them just to satisfy his father's idea of birth order. If anything, that just made him even more determined to do things his own way. In his own time.

Besides, he was content with what he had. Which was Work and…

Work.

He blew out a breath, shifting some files on his desk and setting down his pen. Was he becoming his father, who was so obsessed with work that he ignored everything around him, even the things that were slipping away like his wife and kids?

You don't have a wife or kids, Adem.

He didn't, but he'd put his heart and soul into the starting of this clinic to the exclusion of almost everything else in his life. Including relationships.

It was what he wanted, though. And he had his brother to thank for that. If he'd had the option, he would have named the clinic the Basir Kepler Care Centre, but he doubted his brother would have liked having reminders of what he'd been through. He was truly able to put the past behind him.

Maybe they were different in that as well. Adem and his dad had a strained relationship, even now, whereas Basir worked with their father at the restaurant and would probably own it one day.

Well, no matter. At least he knew Basir would make a wonderful father, judging from what he'd seen of his relationship with Adeline.

The phone on his desk chirped. Glancing

at the screen, he put his pen down. Just who he'd been thinking of. It was his brother.

Flicking the button to take the call, he put it to his ear. "Hi. I hear you have a midwife."

"We do and Addy loves her already. We should actually be there in an hour or so to meet with her again and fill out some paperwork. Can you be there? You might think of something we don't."

"I've never had need of a midwife, Basir."

Ha! Actually, he had, but not quite in the way that his brother meant.

"I know, but you know Carly."

Yes, he did. A little better than he had before. The last thing he needed was to sit in and watch her do Adeline's prenatal appointment.

"I don't know. I'm pretty busy."

"Come on, Adem. We're excited and wanted to share it with family. You work right there at the clinic."

"Okay, I'll make it work."

Somehow. He just wasn't sure quite how

he was going to face Carly and not see the imprints of her hands against his living room window all over again.

Carly was nervous, and she wasn't sure why. It wasn't the first time family members had sat in on an appointment and it wouldn't be the last. In fact, Basir and Adeline had requested this meeting after researching birthing options.

But this was Adem.

As much as she tried to tell herself it was because he was the head of the clinic and that he would be looking at her through that lens, she knew that wasn't entirely it. More of it involved having him here while they discussed birth plans. She couldn't stop herself from wondering what kind of birth experience he would choose for his own child. Would he be involved? Or detached? Would he want his partner to have a hospital birth or one at home?

She had a hard time suppressing the tiny pang that went through her at the fact that she would probably never know. Nor should she.

And if he got married and asked her to play a role in his own wife's pregnancy?

It was a completely irrational thought, but one she couldn't entirely banish. Of course he wouldn't ask.

But if he did?

She wasn't sure she could do it, and she didn't really understand why.

And that was her cue to get back to the business at hand.

"We'll have most of our prenatal appointments here at the clinic until we get closer to your due date. Then nearer the date, I or one of my team will visit you at home. We need to have at least one appointment there, anyway, so we can put everything in place. You mentioned on the phone that you've done some research on types of home births."

Adeline nodded. "We have and wanted to hear your opinions, since we're leaning toward a water birth. Since Adem's a neurosurgeon, we thought it would be good to hear his thoughts as well."

Out of the corner of her eye, she saw him stiffen. "I'm sure Carly can guide you through those decisions."

Was he afraid she would be offended that they'd asked him to be here? Nothing could be further from the truth. Glancing over, she said, "I welcome whatever input you might have."

"I am not a birth expert."

Basir spoke up. "No, but you're family. And an expert in your field, and since we've chosen something a little less conventional, we really do want to hear your opinion."

"Water births have been around for a long time," Carly said. They were growing in popularity actually. "We'll need to work out some things, but that is very possible as long as your pregnancy is progressing without complications. We'll do an ultrasound to make sure there's only one baby in there, since we wouldn't want to go that direction with twins either."

"And you've assisted with water births before?" Adeline's voice was soft, her happiness obvious.

"Yes. We even have a birthing pool here at the clinic, which brings me to another question. Where would you get your pool?"

This time Basir answered. "That was part of our research. We found a company we can buy a new one from. We can either keep it for future pregnancies or they'll sell it for us once we're done. They have guidelines set up for how to do it all." He handed her a card.

She glanced at the name. "I've worked with them before. They're very reputable."

"That's a relief."

Basir glanced at his brother. "This is where you come in. What is your take on water births?"

"Are you asking me as a doctor?"

"I am. Since the baby will be born underwater, will there be any problems as far as oxygen? I know everyone says they're perfectly safe, but we just want to make sure."

Carly could have answered that question, but she understood why Basir wanted reassurance from an objective party. Not that Adem was, since he was also family.

"Carly is probably better off answering that question. But if you're worried about oxygen deprivation, there won't be any, since the baby will be still attached by the cord."

"Water birth babies are only submerged for a matter of seconds once they're born, so Adem is right, there's no danger in that regard. But I would hold off on buying an actual birth pool until you're a little further along, just so we can make sure everything is running according to plan."

"How far along?"

"I'm going to say six months. We only want to go that route under optimal conditions, for your sake and the baby's."

Adeline nodded. "I do understand that. And since Adem seems to be in agreement, let's plan on that."

When Carly shot him a look, he was

frowning and didn't look very happy. Was he not a fan of water births? Again, it didn't matter, since this wasn't his baby. But as director of the clinic, it might be good to know his stance, since Carly was a proponent of the method.

Fifteen minutes later, they'd finished their discussion and Carly bid them both goodbye. But when Adem looked like he was going to shoot through the door behind them, she asked him to hold up.

When the door of the exam room closed, she got straight to the point. "Do you have a problem with your brother and his wife wanting a water birth?"

"Why do you ask?"

"I'm not sure. You just looked less than pleased once they firmed up their decision."

"It's not my child."

"No, but it is your niece or nephew. And your attitude will make itself known sooner or later. Besides, I would personally like to know what you think."

"Why?"

The way he said that made her hesitate. Then she decided she really did need to know. “Because you’re the clinic’s director. I’d like to make sure you stand behind our patients who choose to have their baby in a pool.”

“Of course. It’s just such a different field. I’m a neurosurgeon, so the idea of performing brain surgery in someone’s home is unfathomable to me. But it’s not brain surgery and obviously some people are more comfortable giving birth in familiar surroundings.”

“Yes, that’s right. They do. Okay, I just didn’t want Basir and Adeline to start down this road only to be sidetracked by some objection you might have.”

“Believe me, if I’d had one, you would have known it.”

“Well, that’s good to know.”

His head cocked. “Anything else?”

“No. That was all.”

“Okay, so now that we have that out of the way, I’ll see you later.”

She nodded and watched him walk out of the room, unsure of why she'd gone from nervous to defensive to deflated in less than an hour's time.

That wasn't quite true. She did know why. She just didn't like the reasons for it. Because they involved a man she was afraid was becoming a little too important in her life. He made her pulse soar and her heart trip in her chest. And yet he'd shown no interest in repeating their night together. Or having a relationship of any sort with her.

Lord, she'd already survived one man walking out on her. The last thing she needed to do was set her poor heart on a shelf and wait for it to be knocked down again. Because she had a feeling this time it wouldn't bounce, but would instead shatter into a million pieces.

CHAPTER FIVE

ADEM'S LIFE HAD been so busy he'd barely had time to stop and breathe since the news of Adeline's pregnancy and Basir's question about water births being safe. The question seemed even more poignant this morning as another family faced a horrific choice.

There'd been a string of emergencies related to a terrible pileup on the M1 a week ago. Three fatalities and dozens of injuries, including nine traumatic brain injuries. Adem had either treated or consulted with other hospitals on most of them.

And today he'd had to stand at the bedside of a five-year-old child and listen as her family begged him to find some sign of hope on her EEG readings. But there were none. After the accident, her brain swelled, continuing unabated despite his team's every attempt to stop it, including a craniotomy—removing a piece of her skull to relieve pressure. Nothing worked, and in the early hours, her brain stem had herniated.

At this point the ventilator was the only thing keeping their daughter's body alive. And seeing her mother, also injured in the crash, sit there with a cast on her arm and plead for her daughter's life had wrenched him in a way that he wasn't used to. Unlike Carly, who was deeply involved with her patients for nine months, Adem was able to maintain more emotional distance from his. Whether that had to do with his training or with his upbringing was up for debate.

Whatever it was, he was having a harder time coping today.

The organ donation team was on standby, waiting for a chance to talk to the family. It all seemed so cold-blooded right now, even though he knew he wasn't thinking rationally.

He couldn't imagine being a parent and having to face the death of your child. Hadn't cared about anyone enough to even think of having a family with them. At least until Basir entered the picture with his news. But his brother was happily married. Adem was not, and since there was no one on the horizon, there would be no children in his foreseeable future. He would not make the same mistake his parents had made and bring kids into a less than ideal partnership.

He sighed. Why were those thoughts going through his head today?

Adem had faced other heartbreaking outcomes with patients, but rarely with someone so young. Realizing he'd been staring out of his office window for the last fifteen minutes, he swiveled his chair back toward the front and planted his elbows on his desk. Steepling his hands, he rested his forehead on his fingertips, trying to pull his mind toward other things, even as that child's family was now grappling with the hardest choice a parent would ever have to make.

A knock on his door sounded.

Damn. Here it was. He'd given them his mobile number and asked them to call him, but maybe someone had directed them here. Maybe they wanted to ask him to run more tests. Didn't they know if there was any possibility…the tiniest sliver of hope…? He drew a deep breath and stood, going over to the door and opening it.

Not the family. Or anyone else involved with the case. It was Carly.

He couldn't imagine why she was here. Wait. "Is it Adeline?"

"No. Naomi."

Hell, their aneurism patient. He suddenly couldn't take one more failure. Maybe she saw something in his face, because she put her hand on his arm. "No, she's okay. More than okay. She had her baby this morning. They delivered by C-section and everyone is great. Not a hint of trouble from the aneurysm. The coiling worked."

He blinked. "That's the best news I've heard today. In fact, it's pretty much the only good news I've had."

"The accident?"

"You heard?"

Her head tilted. "It's been all over the news. You were even on television."

He remembered a gaggle of reporters gawking at him last night as he'd left the building, but it was all a blur. All he'd been able to think about was that little girl and the fact that he wasn't going to be able to save her.

"I don't remember talking to anyone."

"No, they just showed a video clip of you walking to your car and saying that your quick thinking had helped save lives at two different hospitals."

"Kahretsin." A dagger speared through his skull. "Not all of them."

An hour. They'd asked for an hour alone with their daughter before making any decisions.

Without being asked, she slid past him and came fully into his office. "What is it?"

He shook his head, throat suddenly too tight to speak.

Carly stared at him for a moment, before shutting the door and taking his hands. "Tell me."

The pain in his chest spread to his jaw, which clenched and unclenched, the muscles in it protesting under the heavy strain. Hell, he was going to break down. Right here in front of her.

Then she let go of his hands and, without saying a word, wrapped her arms around his waist, pressing her cheek to his chest.

They stood there like that for what seemed like an eternity, while he fought to get his emotions under control.

"Adem, it'll be okay."

It wouldn't be. And he wasn't sure it ever would be again. This child was a reminder of what could have happened to Basir during that surgery to remove his tumor all those years ago. Except this wasn't going to end in a child becoming a healthy adult and going on to have a family. Her life stopped right here. Right now.

"I don't think it will. Not this time."

He tipped her face, and even though she had no idea what he was dealing with, those sea-green eyes were moist with unshed tears.

Before he realized what was happening he was kissing her, trying to bury the hideous unfairness of life in the softness of her lips, in the empathy of the arms that still held him.

She kissed him back, hands going to the back of his head and holding him there as if helping him weather the storm that was raging inside of him.

Her feet moved backward, tugging him with her, until she was up against his desk, where the kiss deepened to impossible levels. He wanted her. Right here. Right now. Needed to think about anything else other than what was happening outside his office door.

Lifting her onto the wooden surface, he ignored the sound of his pencil cup falling over, the writing instruments scattering, some of them tumbling off the edge onto the floor.

All he wanted was to feel something. Something that wasn't tragedy. Something that equaled…life.

The life that he felt in her arms. In her touch.

Her hands left his head and went to his belt, undoing it with quick fingers that left him no time to think about anything other than pushing her skirt up around her hips.

And then he was free, and her legs wrapped around the backs of his thighs, dragging him against her, her fingers gripping his already tight flesh.

Just as his tongue speared into her mouth, capturing her moan, she'd somehow connected flesh to flesh with nothing between them.

"Wait." He didn't want to think about anything but her silky skin, the way it felt to be with her, but some tiny rational part of his brain had him digging for his wallet and the tiny packet hidden in there. Especially after that meeting with Basir a week ago.

Then he was sheathed and ready, just as she shifted her body forward. That was all it took. He was inside. Wrapping an arm around her butt, he hauled her against him and buried himself fully.

Ecstasy. That was the only word he could use to describe it. To describe her.

His lips left hers, mouth going to her ear as his breathing roughened. "You're going to send me over, Carly."

Those were the only words he could get out, because her hands pulled him closer, held him tighter. He thrust, the power of the motion scooting her a couple of inches backward. He hauled her against him again, circling his hips to increase the contact between them even as he fought to maintain his own control.

A control that was rapidly slipping.

"Adem…oh! I don't think I can stop…"

A minute later, her body's frantic movements told him all he needed to know. He pulled back, then drove in again, his motions becoming faster, harder, until that emotional release he'd been seeking shot from him, bringing guttural words that made no sense in any language.

And then he was done. Spent. The helplessness and sorrow that had been bottled up inside of him were all washed away. By Carly. It was almost as if she'd sensed his heartbreak and met it in the only way she could.

Gratitude flooded through him, and a strange longing, something he'd never felt before. Just as he started to lean back to smile at her, that little jiggle in the back of his skull turned into an earth-shattering quake. One that could be held back no longer.

He'd done something he'd said he wasn't going to do again. Had sex with her.

"Lanet Olsun!"

He pulled away in a hurry, only to see

confusion on her face, which turned to an uneasy frown.

Then her legs snapped together, and she stood, taking a missed step to the side. He caught her just before she fell. He closed his eyes and curved his palms over her shoulders, head tilting sideways so he could look her full in the eyes.

"I didn't mean to… Carly, I'm sorry."

Her eyes widened. "Don't apologize. I'm as much to blame as anyone." She licked her lips. "It just…happened."

Here. In his office. Where anyone could have walked in, including the parents of that child.

But he certainly wouldn't have done what he did if he'd been thinking straight. But he hadn't been. And Carly's empathy a few minutes ago had obliterated his senses and sent him places he had no business being.

No excuse. Absolutely no excuse. Despite Carly's words, it wasn't her fault. It was his.

And those parents were still sitting by their daughter's bedside.

Sex had changed nothing, after all. Certainly not that. And not the emotions that went along with it. It had merely submerged them for a few quick minutes. Now it was back, and a few other worries bobbed alongside it.

"Hell, it's been a very hard day."

Her mouth tightened ominously. "And I just added to it?"

No. She'd tried to comfort him, and he'd turned it into something else. *He'd* been the one to kiss her. *He'd* been the one to lift her onto that desk. *He'd* been the one who hadn't thought past his own damn needs.

"No, you didn't. But we shouldn't have done this."

"I'm well aware of that." The beginnings of anger appeared in her eyes. "There's no need to keep pounding away at that point."

You'd better zip it, Adem. You're just making things worse.

And if he hadn't got to that condom in time and really screwed things up? Damn, she could have got pregnant.

If she had, would she have told him? Or would she have had an abortion?

The distaste of finding himself with two kids and a loveless union like his parents suddenly fled.

He wouldn't have wanted Carly to have an abortion?

He had no idea. But even condoms sometimes failed.

"Are you on birth control?"

"Um…no. If I remember correctly, you took care of that."

"I did. I just had one screwed-up family growing up. One I wouldn't want to wish on anyone, so I want to make sure that you… that *we* don't—"

"Don't get pregnant? Don't worry, there's absolutely no chance of that." She gave a harsh laugh that cut right through him. "My period is due tomorrow, anyway, so even if we hadn't used something… Well, believe me when I say, I won't get pregnant. I tried once before, but the dice never came up in my favor."

She'd tried to get pregnant?

"I don't understand."

"Neither did I. But it turned out to be for the best."

He touched her hand. "Whatever the reason, I'm sorry."

She stared at him for a long moment. "You have enough on your plate from the sounds of it, without worrying about my problems."

They weren't just her problems, though, they were his. And today his actions, while not exactly reckless, weren't something he was entirely proud of. He'd had impulsive sex, something out of the ordinary for him.

"You'll let me know."

"I'll tell you if something unexpected happens. But I'm sure everything will be fine."

Everything wasn't fine. One day passed, then two. No period. On the third day she woke up with a slight sensation of queasiness that made her frown. There was no way that could be morning sickness. Not with her track record. A year of trying had yielded nothing. Besides, it had only been three days since they'd had sex in Adem's office. Morning sickness took a couple of weeks to develop. At least.

A thought hit her, and she did some quick calculations in her head. Oh, God. What if three days wasn't what she should be worried about? What if three weeks was?

It wasn't three weeks. It had only been two and a half since they'd slept together in his apartment. But they'd used protection all those times.

All those times. There'd been a lot of them.

Think, Carly! There was no possibility that something could have gone wrong? A condom that didn't come off fast enough? Something residual in between times? Something defective?

But how? She and Kyle had tried and tried and nothing had happened. Nothing.

So how was there even the slightest chance that—

Her phone buzzed, making her jump. She glanced at the readout.

Oh, Lord. It was Adem. Probably wondering why she hadn't called to reassure him.

I'm kind of busy right now—trying to reassure myself.

She ignored it, hoping he wouldn't leave her a voice mail. She didn't have an answer for him.

But she could. If she went down and bought a pregnancy test.

Doing so was going to make it pretty plain that she actually was worried about it, when she'd reassured Adem there was nothing to worry about.

And if she was?

How ironic would that be after all this time? She should be thrilled beyond measure. She might still be. She just couldn't wrap her head around it right now.

Her heart stuttered. There was just one catch. Adem did not want a baby. At all.

He'd been extremely quick about asking if she was using additional contraception. And about wanting to know if her period started.

Why? So he could pay for an abortion?

No. That might be right for other people, but it wasn't for her. If she was pregnant, she wanted the baby. Especially after the tears and heartache of trying for so long. But she would make it clear that she expected no help—*wanted* no help—from him or anyone.

Her mom had done just fine after her dad had died. It hadn't been easy for either of them, but her teenage years of growing up with a mother who worked very long hours had fostered a sense of independence that she might not otherwise have.

She could do this. She had a career that she loved, and having a child would only enhance her knowledge of what her patients experienced during pregnancy and labor. And she had her mom.

Yes, her mother would be thrilled, marriage or no marriage.

Dammit.

She didn't need to be jumping ahead to cribs and diapers.

Just go and get the test, Carly, and then worry about Adem and all the other stuff later.

An hour later, she had her answer, and despite her earlier thoughts, it wasn't the one she was expecting. It also confirmed when it had happened. Her hormone levels wouldn't be high enough after only three days to register on a home test. But they would after three weeks.

The queasiness grew, helped along by what was quickly becoming panic. Thank God she was off work today. She laid the stick on her bathroom counter and stared at it.

Pregnant.

She was expecting a baby. A baby!

As a midwife, she'd assisted in hundreds of birth. Home births, birthing center births, hospital births, even water births like Basir and Adeline were hoping to have. She'd faced all kinds of situations. But one thing she hadn't had to deal with was a pregnancy of her own.

Looking back, she could honestly say she was glad she hadn't gotten pregnant with Kyle. It might have pushed them into marriage, which probably wouldn't have ended well. No, if she had to do this, she'd much rather do it on her own.

She took her phone and stared at the missed call, which, as she'd suspected, had been from Adem. Her thumb hovered over the name. She'd told him she would let him know if something unexpected happened. Well, this definitely was that. She needed to tell him. It wasn't fair to keep him in the dark. Nor was it possible. She had a feeling her slight nausea wasn't completely caused by nerves, since she'd woken up with it. And Adem was her boss. He saw her at the clinic most days. Kind of hard to hide a growing bump, even under a lab coat.

Call him. Just get it over with.

Except when her thumb mashed a button, it wasn't Adem's phone she was linking to. She was calling the only person she wanted to talk to right now. Her mom.

Three rings later, Madelaine's soothing voice came on the line and her nerves immediately calmed. Her low tones reminded Carly of the cello her mom played so well. She always knew how to talk her off whatever ledge she was on. She would know what to say.

"Hi, Mom. Is there any chance I can meet you for lunch?"

"Of course, honey. Is something wrong?"

Tears sprang to her eyes. She wasn't sure yet if something was "wrong" or if it was just the timing and the partner that was off. All she knew was that she needed some advice from someone that she trusted with her life. She could have called one of her friends from the hospital. Chloe and Esther would both be happy to let her cry all over them. But she didn't want to mar Esther's newfound happiness by sharing her own troubles. And Chloe had been really busy at the hospital lately.

Suddenly she didn't want to wait until they sat in a restaurant to share the news. "I'm pretty sure I'm pregnant."

"Oh, Carolyn, are you sure?" There was a slight pause. "Are you happy about it?"

Her mom only used her full name when she knew Carly was upset about something.

"Yes, I'm sure. And I don't know what I feel just yet. I just found out this morning."

"How far along are you?"

"Only a couple of weeks." There was no way she was going into any more detail than that.

"Why don't you come over to the house. I'll throw together a quiche while you tell me all about it."

"I need to take a quick shower, but then I'll be over." She closed her eyes, and then when she opened them again, a smile formed. "Oh, and, Mom…"

"Yes?"

"Thank you."

"You're welcome. And it's going to be okay."

Her mind clogged with memories. Wasn't that what she'd told Adem that day in his office? Right before she'd welcomed him into herself?

Yes. And as much as she wanted to blame it on that episode, it was pretty obvious her pregnancy had occurred by then. So her words had been a lie. Everything wasn't okay.

Only she hadn't known it at the time.

Well, she needed to shower and drive to her mom's house, which was over by the university where she worked. Hopefully by the time she left there, she would know exactly what she wanted to do. And then she could finally go and confront Adem and tell him the news.

Five hours later, she'd left her mom's house thinking her nerves had finally been put to rest. Her mom was absolutely thrilled. But as soon as Carly got in her car and started driving she found she couldn't stop. Didn't want to go home. She felt prickly and unsettled, and she knew it had something to do with that missed call from this morning. She owed the man the truth.

And if she couldn't screw up the courage to give it to him?

To hell with that. She'd given him her word, and whether she was scared or not, she owed it to him to go in and relieve his mind.

Except she wasn't sure laying something like this on him would constitute relief. At least her nausea was gone. And even though pregnancy tests had given false positives before, she knew in her heart of hearts that this wasn't one of those times.

She would be absolutely devastated if it was actually. After all the railing and tears and pain, she was finally going to get her wish. She was having a baby.

Please don't take this away from me. Please!

She wasn't sure who that question was directed at. Some deity? Or maybe even Adem, who, depending on his reaction, could turn what should be the happiest day of her life into something traumatic.

Well, she was about to traumatize him, wasn't she?

She sighed. It wasn't fair to leave him sitting there wondering. Especially since she'd told him her period was due the day after they were together.

And if he wanted her off Adeline's case for fear it would make things even more complicated?

Complicated for who? Him? Her? He'd said his family relationships were a mess, so there was that. Well, she'd be proactive and offer to step down.

She pulled into a public parking area not far from the university. Taking a deep breath, she went through her missed calls and found Adem's from earlier today. This time she actually dialed his number.

It went to voice mail, and the little bubble of courage popped like a water balloon. Great. She hung up. There was no way she was going to relay this kind of news via voice mail or text. She'd just have to try later. She tossed her phone back into her purse, only to hear it immediately start ringing. She gulped. It was him. It had to be.

She scrabbled in her purse to find the errant phone, pulling it out just as a third ring sounded. She quickly hit the button to answer and put the phone to her ear. "Hello?"

"Carly. Sorry. I left my phone in the office at the clinic to get water to make coffee and it had just finished ringing when I got to it."

She remembered the small silver pot he'd had that day in the cafeteria. That was what had gotten this whole thing started. She'd never even gotten to try it, and after today, it was likely she never would. Once he heard the news, he'd probably want nothing more to do with her, especially if she wasn't open to terminating the pregnancy. Surely he wouldn't even suggest it after what she'd shared with him. Even if he did, there was no way…

She would just make it very clear that she was fine raising this child on her own.

"It's okay. Listen, is there somewhere we can meet?"

There was a long silence on the phone, making her heart cramp. Had he already guessed what this was about? "I take it you're not at the clinic right now. Do you want to come in or meet at my apartment?"

No. She suddenly knew she needed it to be somewhere other than one of those places. Somewhere neutral. She glanced up and saw a sign for Hyde Park. Why not there?

"How long before you finish up at work?"

"Just tying up a few loose ends, then I'm free."

And I'm about to give you a whole lot more loose ends. Ones that can't be tied up in a day or even a few weeks.

Should she ask him about the patient he

was so upset about the other day? No. She was pretty sure there had not been a happy ending in sight. There had been a desperation in his kiss that she hadn't recognized. It made what happened a lot more understandable. He'd been distraught, and she'd been a welcome distraction.

A distraction. She was pretty sure that made what she was about to tell him even worse.

Adem had a reputation for keeping his business life strictly separate from whatever life he had outside of the clinic. None of the women there ever claimed to have slept with him or even dated him. So either he didn't date at all, or…

But he'd earned that reputation somehow. And he'd known exactly how thick that glass was.

There were a few other hints that the man didn't live completely like a monk. But she was pretty sure if he'd had a steady relationship, she would have heard about it at some point or other. Not that she'd gone around trumpeting what had happened between them at the clinic.

And a baby? Would the news of who the father was somehow get out?

What a mess.

"Is there any way you could come over to Hyde Park? I'm not far from there now. I can wait."

"Tell me where in the park, and I'll be there."

Carly gave him a spot that she knew could afford them a bit of privacy. She could have suggested one of the nearby restaurants, but she really didn't want anyone to overhear what she had to say. There might be joggers or cyclists in the park, but those folks were normally not interested in anything other than enjoying their surroundings.

She was there within ten minutes, walking down a shaded pathway lined with trees. There weren't as many people here as she expected, but maybe it was the time of day. Coming to the Italian Gardens, where she was supposed to meet Adem, she found a bench facing one of the ponds. Various fountains shot plumes of water into the air, the mists cooling the surrounding area. The portico off to the right featured a Mediterranean-style tile roof and a white stucco finish. All in all, the atmosphere was just what she needed.

She settled back on the bench to wait. Something about the water soothed her senses and maybe even infused a little bit of that lost courage back into her. Calling him had been the worst. And that silence…

She couldn't blame him, and she hated to think about what that drive to Hyde Park was going to be like for him. But telling him was still the right thing to do. And knowing her mom had vowed to help in whatever way she could made her feel…well, not quite so alone, even if Adem wanted nothing to do with the baby.

Stretching her legs out in front of her, she sucked down another cooling breath. If this had happened when she and Kyle were engaged, would it have spurred her into marrying him?

No, and looking back she realized she hadn't been ready for marriage. She still wasn't. She hadn't finished doing the things she wanted to do in life. She enjoyed her freedom, wasn't ready to give that up.

Except a baby would change all of that, anyway, wouldn't it? Yes. In the best possible way. Right now, in this very moment, she was growing a little person inside of her. What she'd thought was impossible had turned out to be very possible. Her hand crept across her belly in wonder, her heart filling with a hope and love she hadn't known existed. How could this possibly be happening?

But it was.

She closed her eyes and concentrated on the light breeze blowing across her body, and the hand on her stomach. No change in the way it felt. Yet. But if things continued to progress, she would soon become aware of it.

Adem hadn't noticed the tiny scars from the laparoscopic surgery she'd had as a teenager, and she hadn't felt the need to tell him the specifics, only that she'd tried to get pregnant and hadn't been able to.

She'd been too caught up in what was happening and in the certainty that the times they'd spent together weren't leading to anything permanent.

Ha! But they had been. Just not the kind of "permanent" she'd been thinking about at the time.

She tilted her head back, trying to enjoy this moment in her life as she listened to the sounds around her. The steady splash of the fountains as water hit water. The twitter of birds in nearby trees. The conversations of people passing her location.

The bench gave a quick lurch as someone sat beside her, and she had to force herself not to jump. It was him. It had to be. Making her movements slow and deliberate, she straightened and opened her eyes, turning to glance at the spot next to her. "Hi."

"Hello, Carly." Adem's dark eyes met hers, the expression in them unreadable. When he glanced at her hand, she realized it was still splayed across her stomach. She quickly moved it back to her side.

So how did she do this? Blurt out the news in the same way you would rip an adhesive dressing off a wound?

The way he was looking at her made her decide against that. She didn't want to add more stress onto whatever else he was dealing with today.

He saved her the trouble. "I take it your period didn't arrive, despite what you said."

Gulping, she shook her head. "No. It didn't. I had a little queasiness, so I decided to go ahead and take a pregnancy test."

"There's no way it could register that quickly."

"You're right. It couldn't. But it could after almost three weeks."

Was it her imagination or was there a quick flash of relief that crossed his face?

"I haven't been with anyone else, if that's what you're wondering."

The look fled in an instant. God. Had he actually thought—hoped—she might be carrying someone else's child?

"I guess I was right worrying about additional protection."

She clasped her hands in her lap. "I really didn't think it was possible. Not with my history."

"Cehennem."

The word rolled off his tongue and passed through her gut with a shivery sense of doom. "I don't know what that means."

Whatever he'd just said was nothing like those sexy words he'd muttered in Turkish during their times together.

"Sorry. I just never wanted… So the test came back positive."

He never wanted what? To have children? Her insides clenched.

"It did."

He blew an audible breath. "I see. What do you want to do?"

"I'm glad you phrased it that way. This is my issue. I don't expect you to do anything. It's my decision, and I want to have this baby. I need to have this baby."

"Why?"

The question was so quick in coming that she didn't have time to formulate a coherent answer. Instead, the truth came tumbling out in a rush. "I told you I tried to have a baby. It was with my fiancé. But it never worked, even after a year. We broke up soon afterward."

"Did you get checked out?"

"No. I already knew the reasons. I had a twisted ovary when I was younger. It had to be removed, so that left me with one. Which should have been enough. But it wasn't. I assumed I would never have a baby." She looked at him. "But here I am."

"Yes. Here you are."

He still hadn't said how he felt about it. "Like I said, I don't expect—"

"This is my baby too. Of course I want to be part of his or her life. I *will* be a part of it. I just can't… I can't do the whole marriage thing."

She turned toward him in an instant, trying to ignore the quick sting of hurt. "I never said *anything* about marriage. I don't *want* to get married. At all. I was engaged once, and it was a disaster. You said you wanted to know…about the other. So I felt you should know."

Evidently he hadn't expected quite that vehement a response because he stopped her with a rueful-looking grin. "Okay, okay. I didn't realize I was that unattractive a catch."

She couldn't hold back a smile of her own, very glad he didn't seem furious that she was keeping the baby. "I didn't realize I was that terrible of a catch either."

He touched her face, one finger sliding down her jawline in a way that made her shiver. "Like I told you, my family is a mess. Believe me, you're a very good catch. For a man who is better than I am. Marriage and permanent relationships just don't seem to be in the cards for me."

"I'm sure if the right person comes along..."

"Doubtful." He gave a half-shrug, dropping his hand as one ankle came to rest on his knee. He looked over the water in the distance. "Anyway, if you're going to have this baby, I intend on being there."

"Like I said, there's no need. My mom is great, so I have a wonderful support system."

"Hmm. That's something I'll have to think about."

She tilted her head in question.

"About how to tell my folks. They're very old-fashioned. I love them, but we don't always see eye to eye about certain things. Basir...well, he seems to have a monopoly on happiness in our family. And I'm very glad for him."

"I'm serious, Adem. You don't have to play any role you don't want to play."

He turned back toward her. "But it

wouldn't be a role, like in a play, would it? I am actually going to be a father. And yes. I am going to be part of his or her life. I just need to think through how to go about it."

What did that mean? That he was going to throw money at the baby, without actually spending time with his child? She needed to make something pretty clear to him right up front. "I don't want or need your money. And I also don't want some kind of benign uncle who will slide in and out of the baby's life. I want stability—the kind that I had growing up. Either you're known as his or her father or you can bother not showing up. I'm not going to lie or pretend otherwise."

He touched her arm. "Hey, I didn't mean that at all. I just need some time to sort through the logistics of it. It's going to change a lot. Maybe even our working relationship."

"Why? People have children together all the time."

He dropped his hand back to his side.

"Yes, but I'm heading up the clinic. I don't want rumors swirling around about what happened between us. So I need to decide if I have to step down or not before this gets out."

Horror washed through her. She hadn't even thought about that possibility. She'd been worried about the changes to her own life and hadn't even stopped to think that it might change things for him as well. She'd assumed as long as he knew she didn't expect marriage or much of anything from him that life could pretty much go on as usual. "No! I don't want you to do that. There's no reason to."

"I think there might be. You work for the clinic, and I head it up. If the information were twisted in just the right way…"

"I wasn't planning on shouting the baby's parentage from the rooftops. I understand this is a huge deal, but…" She clasped her hands. "You do good work at the clinic, Adem."

"So do you."

"Do you want *me* to resign?" Lord, she didn't want to do that. She loved her job. Loved helping people like Naomi. The stress that she'd released into the universe came crashing back down onto her shoulders.

"No. The fact is, we shouldn't have slept together in the first place. And since there are always consequences for actions, I need to be willing to face them." His eyes dropped to her abdomen for a second before coming back up. "For what it's worth, I'm glad you're keeping the baby. And happy that you were able to get pregnant. Truly. Just give me a few days to process things."

She nodded her agreement, even as her brain tore through the possibilities. He could step down, which would devastate her. He could decide to keep the baby's parentage a secret. Which would also devastate her.

Or he could decide that the reward was worth the risk and parent this child alongside of her.

She already knew which choice she was hoping for. She just wasn't so sure Adem would be willing to walk out on that limb and risk having it breaking off behind him.

CHAPTER SIX

OVER THE NEXT WEEK, Adem vacillated between optimism and dread. He and his brother had grown up in a household filled with tension. What he'd told Carly had been the tip of the iceberg.

Once his brother's health improved, his dad hadn't been around much, needing to spend the time on his fledgling restaurant, and his mum had seemed relieved by his long work hours. And when they were together, the chilly silences were worse than any fight could have been. They smiled and said the right things when they were out in public, but they were both miserable, and because of their deep-rooted belief in duty, they refused to take the obvious way out.

Despite all of that, his knee-jerk response toward the news that Carly might be pregnant was the M word. But because it had kept rushing to the tip of his tongue, even though he knew in his heart of hearts that it would be the wrong thing to do, he carefully and deliberately told Carly that marriage was off the table. He'd seen the instant flash of hurt that went through her eyes before she countered his words by saying that she didn't want to get married either.

He believed her. That kind of vehemence wasn't feigned. She'd said she'd had a failed engagement, maybe that was part of the reason. So at least she could understand what was at stake. But despite all the rational reasons for not getting married, he'd been surprised to find that her words actually did sting. Damn.

The pregnancy was definitely not planned. But, according to Carly, not unwanted.

His younger brother was ecstatic over the fact that he and Adeline were having a baby. Maybe like Carly, he'd wondered if it were even possible because of his tumor. He'd never talked about the fear of it coming back, but he wouldn't be human if it hadn't at least crossed his mind. But despite all of that, Basir had been willing to plunge into those waters and accept the challenges of fatherhood with joy.

Adem was not his brother. And he'd spent a lot of time as a teenager stepping in to provide the things he felt were lacking in their household. And he'd got rid of his own anger as a result.

His brother seemed fairly well-adjusted. Or, maybe as Carly had said, he'd just found the "right" person. The person who could erase childhood wounds.

Adem had no desire to erase them. Or to try to bypass them only to discover he'd been wrong. He wanted no child of his to grow up in the kind of atmosphere that he had. So the kindest thing he could do for this baby was to take a step back and make sure history did not repeat itself.

Hadn't he already wondered if his many hours spent at work didn't mimic his father's blinkered approach to life? Marriage might even make that worse, causing him to retreat to old patterns when things went badly.

Adem didn't even know if he was capable of a healthy relationship.

He got up from his desk and decided to go for a walk to clear his head. As soon as he made it to the front of the clinic, he encountered a couple of familiar faces. Naomi with her husband, daughter and baby in tow were walking across the foyer. Carly came out of a bank of white mini-offices and smiled at them, ushering them toward her cubicle.

Unable to resist, he started toward the group. Carly spotted him first, and the smile that was on her face faded.

He'd caused that. And he hated it. He remembered his dad's unexpected appearances at home doing much the same thing.

Ignoring her look of dismay, he smiled at the couple and Naomi waved, waiting for him to catch up. "How are you, Mr. Kepler?"

"I'm well." He shook their hands, including Tessa's. "How are you? Adjusting to having a newborn?"

He hadn't meant it as a jab, but Carly stiffened almost immediately.

Douglas held his finger below his left eye, tugging down the lower lid. "Does this tell you anything? We adopted Tessa when she was nearly two, so we got to bypass the nighttime feeds and nappy changes."

Despite the bloodshot eyes, the new father seemed ecstatic with their newest family member.

Naomi shifted the bundle in her arms and swatted at her husband's arm. "You're not the one feeding her in the middle of the night."

"I'm not equipped to do that." He grinned. "But seriously, Doc, you should try it sometime. There's nothing like seeing this little person you helped create look at you for the very first time."

Of their own volition, Adem's eyes went

to Carly, whose face looked a little more pink than it normally did.

"I'm sure it's special."

"Yes. It is. And we're so grateful—to both of you—that Naomi is healthy again."

"I'm glad as well. Any other problems? The headaches are gone?"

Naomi nodded. "Completely. I don't know how to thank you."

"Thank Carly. She's the one who asked me to take a look. She could have just told you to take a couple of ibuprofen."

"Naomi might not be around if that had happened. Neither would Charlotta."

Adem smiled. "Is that her name? It's beautiful. Can I see her?"

The baby's face was hidden in a layer of blankets. Naomi carefully peeled them back and revealed a cute week-old baby with a full head of dark hair. She was wide awake, her curious gaze trying to focus on her surroundings.

The couple's other daughter, who clutched her dad's neck, said, "Lotta likes me."

"Yes, she does," Douglas said. "Your baby sister loves you."

"I love her too."

A pang hit Adem as he glanced at Carly. Would she try to have more kids after this one was born? If so, who would she have them with? God help him, he couldn't even picture her with anyone else.

Except him.

That wasn't going to happen.

"I was just going to take them back to an exam room so I could see how Naomi's doing." Carly's tone was a little more brusque than he expected. But then again, they hadn't really talked about what had happened since that day in the park. Oh, they'd exchanged pleasantries, but just in passing. They were eventually going to have to sit down and hammer out some real details and decide what the other's expectations were.

Expectations? Did he even have any?

Damn. He was starting to think he did, and that wasn't good. Maybe that was part of the reason he'd buried himself in work over the last several days.

Double damn.

Yes, they needed to figure this out. Now was obviously not the time. But when?

"I'd like to do a follow-up MRI as well, to make sure that aneurysm is completely sealed off. I'll put in an order for it, if that's all right with you."

"I'm breastfeeding—will it affect that?"

"No. I'll double-check with the pediatrician at the hospital, but I've had a couple of other patients who've needed contrast dye. At the time, the recommendation was that it didn't require an interruption in breastfeeding."

Douglas spoke up. "Then we want it done."

His wife laughed. "Thanks for giving me some input." She glanced at Adem. "Yes, of course. You have no idea how much better I feel after having the procedure. Have you done a lot of them?"

"Quite a few. And yours went very well."

He smiled. "I'll let you get back to your appointment. Carly, could I speak to you for just a minute?"

"Of course. Let me just get them in a room." She'd hesitated long enough before answering to let him know she really didn't want to talk to him. Or maybe she just thought it was inappropriate for him to approach her about it at the clinic. Well, he wasn't going to discuss the pregnancy itself right now; he just wanted to set up a time when they actually could talk about it.

She'd acted like she didn't care who knew, that she wasn't going to lie about who the baby's father was. Maybe she'd changed her mind about that.

After she'd closed the door, she nodded toward an area off to the right, where there was an empty office. Since it was later in the day, no one was in any of the chairs. She sat in one, and he sat across from her. "Okay, I'm listening."

"Now that we've both had some time to

think, I'd like to discuss things again. Everything is still the same?"

So much for merely suggesting a time and a place.

"Yes. I'm still pregnant, if that's what you're asking. But…" She paused again. "I really don't want this to affect you, Adem. I didn't give you much of a choice, and even if you'd wanted me to terminate, I would have refused. So…now I'm giving you an out."

He blinked. Then frowned. "I think I made it pretty clear that I didn't want an out. That I was ready to accept the consequences—whatever they are."

"Consequences. That makes it sound like a punishment of some sort."

"I didn't mean it like that."

"I can see how it might seem that way, though. At least to you. So let's just keep things quiet. I'm not going to advertise that I'm pregnant until it becomes pretty obvious. And if someone asks me who the father is, I'll just say he's out of the picture."

Oh, hell, no. Whatever else Adem might have thought, he had no intention of just fading away. Especially not after seeing the joy Charlotta had brought to Douglas's face.

He swallowed, picturing her with an abdomen swollen with child. *His* child.

"And when she runs to me and grabs my legs at the clinic? Will you say the father's out of the picture then?" He leaned in closer. "Because I'm telling you right now, I plan on being very much in the picture."

"Did you say 'she'?"

"He or she. These are all things I'd like to talk about, before people start asking questions."

She nodded. "I agree. It's just hard to know what to do right now. I'll deny you're the father until my dying breath if you say you're going to step down as the director. Victoria Clinic needs you."

"It needs you too, Carly. But no one person is irreplaceable."

"Tell that to your child after it's born."

"Touché. Okay, tell me where you want to meet, and we'll figure this out."

"I don't have a clue, but definitely not here at the clinic. Or at the hospital."

He thought of something. "Listen, my parents have a boat at a marina on the Thames. We could get away, where there's no chance of anyone overhearing us." He paused. "You said you were queasy the last time we spoke. Maybe that would be a problem."

"Actually, I love being out on the water. When I was younger in the States, we used to do these white-water rafting tours."

"I don't think we'll encounter anything like that on the Thames, since there are speed restrictions everywhere. We likely won't get very far. But the boat has a cover, and we could take a lunch with us. Not to pressure you or anything. I just want to work through things while…you…are still in the early stages."

"Okay." She smiled. "That sounds fun. As long as your parents don't mind."

"It's a family boat. My brother and I have

both used it before, but I don't see Basir and Adeline wanting to go out with everything else that's going on. But if there's a problem, I'll let you know, okay?"

She stood. "Okay. Let me at least bring the food, since you're providing the boat."

"How about I give you a call in a few days and we can nail that down along with a date." He stood as well.

"Sounds good." Her hand brushed his in a light touch. "And for what it's worth, I don't regret everything that happened."

His lips curved as she walked away from him and said in a voice too low for her to hear, "Neither do I, Carly. Neither do I."

And he realized for the first time since she'd told him the news, he really meant it.

Carly had opted to meet him at the marina, three days later, rather than have him stop by her place to pick her up and she wasn't sure why. Was she afraid to have him over?

Um, that would be a resounding yes. Despite her insistence that what had happened between them was over, there'd been a subtle buzz of anticipation ever since he'd mentioned going out on the boat. If she'd thought Adeline's pregnancy was going to connect her and Adem's lives on a temporary basis, what was having a baby of their own going to mean?

And what about the way she'd reached for his hand and told him she didn't regret what had happened?

Was that true?

Lord help her, yes, it was. As hard as she tried to fight off her feelings for him, they were relentlessly growing. And she wasn't sure how to stop them.

It had to be the baby. Or hormones. Or something other than the fact that the man was eating away at her defenses without even trying.

She still wanted him physically as well, which made it even worse. But Carly did not see herself as a "friends with benefits" kind of person. Were they friends?

She thought they might be heading in that

direction…before the pregnancy had happened. And now? She didn't know. What she felt for Adem seemed to blur the boundaries she'd drawn for herself. Well, there was one way to sharpen those lines again.

She could assert her independence and make sure he knew that, ultimately, she called the shots with this baby.

And when she runs to me and grabs my legs?

As soon as he'd said those words, she'd pictured a little girl with dark pigtails and Adem's smile running toward him, arms opened wide. It was an image she hadn't been able to banish.

It had replayed in her head time and time again, becoming clearer and clearer.

Which made it all the more important to put a cleaver between "want" and what was best. For her. For their child.

And yet here she was, picnic hamper in hand, getting ready to go out on a boat with him. And that anticipation was still there, rumbling in the background, growing stronger by the minute.

It's not a lover's gondola, Carly.

Really? Meat, cheese, grapes—the things she'd brought for their meal? Weren't those the things that were normally eaten in intimate settings?

Not in this case.

Adem appeared on the dock, dark hair ruffling in the breeze, wearing dark brown shorts, those tanned legs sporting the kind of lean muscle that made her mouth water. Her anticipation revved up a couple of notches, becoming the roar of outboard engines.

Independence, Carly, remember?

She suddenly felt self-conscious in a pink sundress that exposed pale calves and white feet. Thinking about it, her leather thong sandals were probably not the best choice of footwear for a boat either. But it was too late now, and like he'd said, they weren't likely to go far with the speed restrictions.

He came up beside her and took the basket. "I'm glad you came."

"I told you I would."

"Yes, you did. I wondered if you actually would, though."

She forced a smile. "You'll find I keep my word."

"So do I."

A reference to when he told her to make no mistake, that he would be a part of his baby's life?

This conversation could get very sticky very quickly. She decided to change the subject to something a little more neutral. "Where's the boat?"

"Halfway down the dock on the right. The *Ankara*."

"Named after the city?"

"It's where my parents were born." He walked beside her as they made their way across the plank walkway where boats bobbed on either side of them. "Where they were married."

"How long have you lived here in the UK?"

"I was fifteen when my dad moved us here."

She didn't know that. But it made sense. "Wow, his restaurant must be fairly successful, since he owns a boat like this."

"Yes. He works very hard. In that he's successful."

But not in other things? He'd said his family was a mess.

Was that why he wanted to be a part of his child's life? To fulfill something that he thought was lacking in his own upbringing? She had no idea, and right now she was afraid to ask. She wanted him to love his child for who he or she was, not because it was a means to an end.

The bubble of anticipation deflated just a bit.

He'd mentioned before that he wasn't sure how he was going to tell his parents, which further supported the idea that things were strained in the family.

The *Ankara* was where he said it would be. All white with sharp black lettering, the boat was immaculate. It wasn't a yacht, but it was bigger than what she'd pictured in her head. With a white canvas cover that stretched from the steering wheel to about halfway back, there were four seats in the shade and four behind that, where passengers could catch some sun.

Adem stepped across onto the boat, set the hamper on one of the seats and then held his hand out to her. She hesitated before gripping his fingers and letting him help her aboard. As the touch continued to linger, she was hyperaware of every inch of his skin against hers.

Lord, hadn't she read that pregnancy could make her crave things? Like what they'd done in his flat? But that wasn't supposed to happen until the second trimester. And in actuality, that craving had been there long before she'd ever become pregnant. If she'd hoped it would magically disappear, she was clearly mistaken.

It was very much alive and well.

She hopped on the boat and let go of him in a hurry, afraid he might somehow guess her thoughts.

"I like your dress."

His smile made her heart trip a time or two. So much for trying to change her train of thought. That evidently wasn't going to happen.

"Thanks. I don't think I've ever seen you in shorts."

His smile turned crooked. "I won't remind you of what you have and haven't seen me in."

God, there was that. She'd seen him in a whole lot of nothing. But reminding her of that fact wasn't going to help either of them. Especially since she was now picturing him without those shorts.

She decided to let that comment pass without a reply.

Picking up the basket, he made his way to the covered area where the steering wheel and controls were, not that she was familiar with nautical terms. "It's turned out to be a really nice day."

"It has. We can unzip the front portion of the cover to let the air blow through, once we stop, otherwise it'll get pretty warm under here."

"I can imagine." She was getting warmer by the minute, in fact.

"Ready to go play?" he asked.

She blinked, suddenly picturing that window in his apartment. *God, Carly, he's talking about getting under way, not playing around on the boat. What is wrong with you?*

"I'm ready to head out whenever you are."

With that, Adem undid the mooring lines that kept the boat tied to the dock, then started the engines. Minutes later, they were out of the marina and moving onto the Thames itself.

There were stairs leading to an area somewhere below deck. Probably sleeping quarters and maybe a galley kitchen. People routinely slept on their boats in the States, where boating was a big business, but she wasn't sure if things were the same here.

She wasn't going to ask for a tour, though,

that was for sure. Because seeing a bed would send her thoughts floating back to another kind of tour. And that was one word she avoided like the plague nowadays.

Instead, she settled in and tried to enjoy the sights on the waterway amid the throb of the engines and the traffic of other boaters. She wasn't sure of their destination, and right now she didn't care.

Adem glanced over. "How are you feeling? I know you said you weren't sick, but I didn't think to ask about seasickness."

"So far, so good." The conditions seemed pretty smooth. If anything, it was exhilarating to be away from the hospital. He'd been right about that. She needed to cut loose and have fun sometimes. She hadn't realized it until she'd spent that night with him. It was one of the few times her mind hadn't been crammed full of thoughts of patients. Maybe that was part and parcel of being a midwife, since one of her patients could go into labor at any minute. Even while she was here on a boat. She glanced down at the screen of her phone, half expecting to see that that had indeed happened, but so far there was nothing there, other than a text from her mom asking if she was free for lunch on Friday. She picked it up and started to reply.

"No work allowed."

Carly crinkled her nose. "I can't exactly schedule when my patients go into labor, you know. And right now my life is free enough that I can easily get away."

"Not right this second, unless you jump overboard."

She laughed. "That's not what I meant, and you know it." She enjoyed this light and easy chatting, felt like she hadn't done this with him in ages, if ever.

"I do. But I also know that soon your life is about to get a lot more complicated."

What? Oh, he meant with her pregnancy. So much for light and easy. But he was right. Things were going to change drastically. Something she didn't want to think about right now. She decided to change the subject. "Where are we going, anyway?"

"There's a little marina I have in mind. It'll take us about an hour to arrive." He nodded toward shore. "Look, the Eye."

She hadn't realized they would pass the London Eye, and it looked bigger somehow from the water. Strangely, she had never been on the iconic Ferris wheel. Maybe because she wasn't really a fan of heights. And then she found herself searching for his apartment building.

Her fear of heights certainly hadn't bothered her that time. Maybe because her mind had been a lot more wrapped up in what he was doing to her.

In more ways than one.

She glanced to her belly, her mouth twisting in a sardonic smile.

What were they going to do?

She had no idea. She was still dwelling on those thoughts when Adem throttled down the engines, pulling into a section of the river where there were all types of boats moored, from large sailboats to vessels much smaller than Adem's family's boat.

Wow, an hour had gone by already. Despite the slow speed, she'd enjoyed puttering down the river.

She got up and, under his direction, helped him secure the boat in one of the berths, tossing some kind of padded bolster things over the side. "What are these called?"

"Fenders."

She leaned over and felt one of them. "I would have guessed bumpers."

"Well, they serve the same purpose. Thanks for the help."

She hated to admit it, but it was fun. There was a weird camaraderie between them that she'd never really experienced before. Not even with Kyle.

She realized she'd been on the defensive with Adem more often than not in most of their earlier dealings. When had that started changing? Maybe with Naomi and her aneurism?

She wasn't sure. But something had definitely shifted.

Maybe because you slept with the man, Carly.

Was that really it? She didn't think so. And this baby would link them forever.

Forever.

If someone had told her a year ago that she would be connected to Adem for the rest of her life, she would have said they were crazy.

She hadn't chosen this path, but now that she was here, she was going to make the best of it. So she walked over to the hamper, just as a swell picked the boat up and tilted it a bit.

"Ooops!" She grabbed at the railing, only for an arm to wrap around her waist and haul her against him.

She swallowed and glanced up over her shoulder to see Adem looking down at her, a slight frown on his face. "Are you okay?"

"Just didn't expect the boat to shift when

it did, I guess. Sorry about that. I don't think I would have fallen."

"Sea legs. You'll get them as time goes on."

She wasn't too sure of that, since they were feeling shakier by the minute. But that had nothing to do with the boat and everything to do with the man pressed against her. "Maybe I just need to sit for a second."

He led her over to one of the chairs and stood over her, the frown still in place. "Will you be okay while I go get the air moving?"

A little frisson of contentment went through her, until she thought of those pep talks about being more like her mom. Adem was not always going to be there with her. At least, not like he was right now. "I'm fine. Really."

"Okay, I'll be right back." Adem went to the front and unzipped part of the cover and almost immediately a breeze washed over her. It was luscious. Cooling and refreshing, sliding over her bare shoulders and sifting through her hair.

She tipped her head back. "Oh, that's lovely. So very good."

"Yes, it definitely is."

When she glanced up, he was standing over her, his eyes smoldering with an intensity she recognized from his apartment. Oh, God. She swallowed, trying to calm her heart, which was suddenly racing out of control. "Thank you so much for bringing me out here. I love it."

He dragged a hand through his hair before turning away and grabbing the picnic hamper. "I'm glad. Are you hungry?"

Surprisingly she was. She'd packed extra crackers just in case her morning sickness came back, but so far all was well. "I could definitely eat."

Adem quickly unpacked the basket onto a table screwed into the floor of the boat. Since the small table sat between their two chairs, it almost made it seem like an intimate dinner for two. All they lacked were candles.

Ridiculous. This wasn't some romantic meal. It was a planning session. Better if she remembered that fact.

He set out the plates and the tins of meats and cheeses and fruit. "This looks good."

"In the States fried chicken is the normal fare for picnics, but I guess I've lived in England too long. This sounded more appetizing to me."

"In Turkey it would have been different as well. But you're right. I've become accustomed to life here."

Would being with Adem become as normal as life in London? She couldn't imagine that, but unless he changed his mind, they would be spending a lot of time together outside of the clinic. Would being without Adem feel strange and foreign?

For her sake and his, she hoped not. It would not do to start thinking as if they'd been drawn together by anything other than the baby. If not for that, she would have spent one thrilling night and one naughty day with him. The odds were one of them would eventually leave the clinic and drift toward another job, taking with them the need for continued contact. It had happened with Kyle, despite his promises of them keeping in touch. Not that she wanted to since there was no longer anything binding them together.

Things were different this time, though. Even if she returned to the States at some point in her life, Adem would still be her baby's father. That was never going to change.

"What are you thinking?"

She looked at him. "About how strange it is to be sitting on a boat with you, getting ready to map out a future that I can't even envision at the moment."

"I know."

"What about your parents? Surely this isn't something you can keep from them forever." She couldn't imagine not telling her mom.

He'd said something about them being

old-fashioned. "They wouldn't really expect you to marry me just because of the pregnancy?"

"They came from a culture very different from this one." He glanced over the bow as she dished out the food. "They actually didn't marry for love."

"What?" Oh, God, had they married because his mom had gotten pregnant?

"It was arranged. I know it's hard to understand how things like that can happen from a Western point of view, but there are all kinds of reasons to get married. In their case, it benefited their families."

"Wow. Are they happy?" They had two children together, after all.

"That's a complicated question. They've been together for many years. I'm not sure that constitutes happiness, but it's what they both know. I'm pretty sure my dad has had other women over the years, but I don't know that for sure."

"If that's the case, why would your mom stay?"

"She's the only one who can answer that. All I know is that I'll never follow in their footsteps."

"You're not ever going to get married?"

"I never thought there'd be a reason to."

Before now.

Had that thought just sifted through his mind like it had hers?

"But your brother married." Something about that made her incredibly sad. "What about love?"

"If there is such a thing, I haven't felt it."

Unfortunately for Carly, she was beginning to wonder if she might not be dangerously close to feeling that emotion.

"I believe in it, even though my only serious relationship didn't work out." She was surprised that her breakup hadn't tarnished that belief, but if anything it just made her aware of the need to tread with care around this man. Because the twinges she'd been feeling here and there…

Twinges? Those were more like…

No. Don't think about that right now. The

only kind of love she wanted was the type that a mom had for her baby. The love that she now felt for this little kidney bean she was carrying around inside of her.

His next words interrupted her thoughts.

"Let's talk about the pregnancy. And to answer your earlier question, yes, I will probably have to tell my parents, but I'd rather do that after the baby is born."

The thought of being at home and delivering the baby without Adem in attendance made her swallow. But she had no right to expect him to eagerly offer to be there. She wasn't sure she should even want him there, but she did. And she had no idea why.

Her mom would come. Would even be her birth partner if she asked her to. But Carly wanted more.

"It's going to be pretty obvious to your brother and sister-in-law that I'm pregnant at some point. Unless you want me off the case."

"No. They both want you to deliver the

baby." He blew out a breath. "I have no idea how I'm going to handle any of that."

She screwed up a measure of courage and picked up her fork. One way or another, she needed to know. "Are you even planning on being there when the baby is born? If you're not, I'd rather you tell me now."

CHAPTER SEVEN

BE THERE? WHAT did she mean?

"I've already said I want to be in the baby's life."

She shook her head and speared a bite of meat with her fork, then stabbed the tines through a piece of cheese. The movements were jerky, as if she was really unsure of his answer. "I know, but I'm not talking about that. I mean when he or she is born. Do you want to be there during labor?"

He hadn't thought that far down the road. But some little voice told him to tread carefully, that his answer was important. "Yes. Unless you don't want me there."

Her fork stopped halfway to her mouth and her eyes closed for a split second before looking at him again.

It was the right answer. He saw it in her

face. "What about your parents? You said you didn't want them to know until after the baby was born."

"That might be a little tricky if you decide to have the baby in the hospital where lots of people know both of us."

"I want to have it at home. With just my mom and midwife in the room. And you, if you want to be there."

There was a little tickle of panic in the back of his throat that he did his best to suppress. He'd told her he wanted to be there, but suddenly he wasn't sure. Maybe she didn't want him as a birth partner, though; after all, she said her mother would be there.

And if she did want that? Then there would be birthing classes to attend. Maybe even parenting classes. Together.

It doesn't mean you're marrying her, Adem. Just that you're supporting the mother of your child and ultimately your child.

"How do you feel about me meeting your mother? Before the actual birth?" If he was going to do this, he didn't want to suddenly be thrust into a room with a woman he'd never seen before and hope she didn't resent him for not marrying her daughter. He knew his mother well enough to know that would be exactly her reaction. In fact, she was going to have a hard time understanding why Adem didn't marry Carly.

"Do you want to?"

It took him a second to realize she was answering his question about her mother and not reading his thoughts about marriage. "I think it might be a good idea, don't you?"

"If you're worried about her reaction, don't. I promise you, she's supportive. Thrilled even."

"She'll have to meet me at some point, right?"

"I guess so. I'll check with her and see when a good time might be. But think about it carefully. Once we go down that path, there'll be no turning back. They'll know who you are."

"I think we're already at the point of no turning back. Don't you?"

A smile played at the corners of her mouth. "I think we've been there more than once."

All of a sudden the heat that he'd felt as he watched her enjoy the breeze a few minutes ago returned full force. So did that spark that said maybe marriage was the right answer, after all. "Yes. We have."

Their eyes met. Clashed.

Carly was the first to look away. "I, um, if you're sure about meeting my mom…"

"I am."

"Okay, I'll set it up. Your parents are eventually going to meet me too, when you tell them, right? Are they going to hate me?"

"No. They'll be disappointed with me. Not with you." And they would be. There was no mistaking that. But in the end, it was his life and he'd live it as he saw fit, just as he always had. Just as Basir lived his.

"They'll be mad because you didn't marry me?"

She'd hit the nail on the head. "Yes."

"You could just tell them you tried, but I refused. It wouldn't be a lie, since I did tell you I didn't want to marry anyone. And I don't."

That actually wasn't a bad idea, except for the fact that they would then badger Carly endlessly, trying to talk her into something neither of them wanted. "I don't think that would work. Why don't you let me deal with my parents."

"Sorry. I wasn't trying to interfere." She fiddled with the edge of her plate, making some tiny adjustment. He realized she'd taken his words the wrong way.

He reached across and touched her face, hooking his finger under her chin. "Hey. I know you're trying to help, and I appreciate it. I wasn't telling you to mind your own business. I just don't want to put you in an awkward situation. I would end up having to tell my parents to back off and leave us alone."

"It's okay. And no, I don't want you to

have to do that. We've still got months. Let's give it some time."

"I agree."

With that they were able to move on to lighter topics as they ate, like baby names and what they hoped the child would be like. Carly actually wanted a combined name with influences from both of their home countries.

Adem hoped he or she would look like Carly. The way the light breeze blew her hair off her face, revealing high cheekbones and pale creamy skin. But with his darker skin and dark hair, there would probably be some kind of meeting in the middle. He smiled. He couldn't believe he was actually thinking about things like this.

"Oh, I almost forgot. The portable ultrasounds are going to be delivered next week. The manufacturer is coming over to show us the basics of how to use them. With everything that's going on, I didn't remember to tell you."

"Wow, I had no idea they'd be here this soon."

"I didn't either. I thought it would be a few more weeks. I'll let you know when they want to meet with us."

"Thank you. If I were a little further along, I would offer to be the guinea pig."

"I'm sure we have plenty of patients who'll be happy to volunteer."

"Maybe even Adeline."

"Maybe. I'll run it by her."

She finished her food and took a drink of her water. She'd brought a bottle of wine for him, she said, in case he wanted it. He'd opted for water instead, claiming he still needed to drive the boat home, which he did. But there was also something in him that wanted to keep her company. And that made him take a mental step back.

Was he playing house here?

He'd told her he didn't want a relationship, and he didn't. So what was with the intimate little boat ride? The talking about birth partners and whether he would or wouldn't be in that room when his child was born? All of this had seemed like a good idea at first. Until it didn't. Probably about the time that he realized how beautiful she looked sitting in that chair. How much he wanted to kiss her. To feel her belly at each stage of pregnancy.

These were dangerous games. Ones he had no business playing. Time to put a stop to it.

"Are you ready to head back?"

Maybe she sensed the change in mood, because she wrapped her arms around her waist and said, "Of course. Whenever you are."

Carly acted tough as nails at times, but then there were these little flashes of vulnerability that caught him off guard. And he hated when he was the one who brought them out in her.

Like just now. And when he'd told her he wanted nothing to do with marriage.

But to pretend things were different would just bring heartache of a different kind on down the road. He'd witnessed that firsthand. So, time to put things back on a more even keel.

He helped her stow away the leftovers and secured the basket. Then she helped him pull up the anchor and head back to his home marina.

Carly was quiet on the return trip, but he wasn't sure what he could say or do that would salvage the situation so he decided to let it ride. There'd be plenty of time to figure out the best way to relate to each other when he was a little further from the situation.

Hell, what he meant was a little further from her. Whenever he was around Carly, he didn't seem to be able to think straight. But he needed to figure it out and fast. Before he said something or did something there was no coming back from.

Carly got a call in the middle of the night that one of her patients was in labor. She was exhausted, having been out in the boat for five hours with Adem. An outing that had seemed to start out well, but then at some point he'd become distant, pulling out of that berth in a hurry. He'd barely spoken to her on the way home. Once she sensed the change in him, she went silent as well. They'd said a brief goodbye, and Adem had carried the picnic basket to the car for her. She'd gotten in her vehicle and left as if the hounds of hell were pursuing her. Only they weren't. Neither was Adem. And he'd made that point crystal clear.

She suddenly wasn't sure she wanted to have him meet her mom. Or be at the birth. In fact, she was rethinking a whole lot of things. On a lot of different levels.

Arriving at the house, she found the expectant mom in bed, laboring, her husband beside her, guiding her through her breathing. Touching her. Rubbing her feet, her back—wherever she needed him to be, he was there.

She took a deep breath, trying not to picture Adem doing those things for her. Instead, she forced herself to focus on the situation at hand.

"Hi, Gloria. How are we doing?"

"Good. This feels much the same as our last two children." She gripped her husband Ned's hand. "I don't know what I'd do without him."

"She probably wouldn't be in this predicament if it weren't for me."

Carly smiled, but it wasn't real. The ache she'd had moments earlier quadrupled in size. She'd had this ideal little scenario of her own childbirth experience mapped out in her head. And it looked exactly like this one. Only Carly would be in that bed and Adem would be the one giving her encouraging little touches. Murmuring to her.

She stabbed that dream in the chest, because it wasn't going to happen. If it was anything like the way the day yesterday had ended up being, Adem would be sitting in a chair, while she lay turned away from him, trying desperately not to show him how much she needed his support.

Dammit. She didn't need it. Didn't need him. No matter what her heart might say.

Carly checked Gloria's cervix. Eight centimeters already. And the woman was still optimistic. Which wasn't the norm with a lot of mothers. At some point they usually started turning in on themselves, too caught up in what was going on inside their bodies. But then Gloria and Ned had partnered together for two other children. They had this down to an art.

"I'm just going to get set up. Is there anything you need right now?"

"No. Just some ice cubes. But Ned has those for me."

Right on cue, he scooped up the glass and helped her pick a few out, while Carly got her instruments set up on clean towels on the bedside table.

Maybe she was going to have to swap things out and let her mom be her birthing partner, while Adem simply observed. She wasn't sure she was ready for that level of intimacy with him.

But she'd had such hope.

Was she pinning her hopes on him in other areas as well? Like being there when their child took his or her first steps? Or birthday celebrations? Special milestones?

You're not being fair, Carly. He's still getting used to things.

Just like she was. Maybe instead of just tossing him to the side, she should watch for patterns. If they repeated over and over, then she was going to have some hard choices to make. But now wasn't the time. No one thought clearly at three in the morning.

But she'd better figure out how to put her mind back on her job. For Gloria, Ned and this baby, who was about to make an appearance.

At nine centimeters and fully effaced, excitement crackled as they prepared to bring a new life into the world. Gloria was most comfortable on her side, so Carly let her guide her own delivery. As a midwife, she was there to assist and keep the mom and baby as safe as possible. And if something went sideways, she would take things to the next level. But she didn't expect that to happen in this case.

Ten centimeters. "Okay, Gloria, when you feel the urge to push, you can go ahead."

Ned had opted to stay up by his wife's head to support her and keep her morale high during the process. They made a good team. A team that obviously worked together in a lot of areas of their lives, not just this delivery.

Another thing she wouldn't have in common with Adem.

You work at the hospital with him. That should count for something.

Yes. And she'd worked together with him on Naomi's case.

But was that the same thing? No. But it was either take what they had right now, or nothing at all. There were no other options, so she should stop beating herself and Adem up over something that couldn't be helped.

"I need to push." Gloria's voice broke through her thoughts, and she stopped to put her mind on what was in front of her. Guiding her through fifteen minutes of strong contractions and pushing, the head appeared. Then a shoulder.

Carly eased the presenting shoulder out and then the other. As soon as that happened, the baby slipped out on the next push. She carried the newborn in its towel up to Gloria and Ned. "You have a little girl."

Adem had mentioned having a girl. And they'd talked about the name Derya Ann, which she'd loved as it incorporated both their cultures.

Placing the baby on Gloria's chest, skin to skin, she watched the cord as it continued to pulse.

Ned leaned down to kiss his wife's head. "She's absolutely beautiful. Just like you."

With her free hand, Gloria reached up to pull him back down to her. "She's both of us. We made this beautiful treasure."

Carly's fingers touched her own belly. What Gloria said was true. This couple's new baby wasn't one person or the other. She was both of them. A melding of two identities and genes, and in their case… love.

There was a saying that two out of three wasn't bad. And together she and Adem had made the tiny form that was now nestled safely inside of her.

Their baby.

Why did she keep second-guessing everything? Because she and Adem were nothing like Gloria and Ned. Nothing about the situation made her feel secure, and it bothered her that she even needed that. She was a grown woman who had loved and lost and very nearly lov—

Stop. Just stop.

"Ned, the cord has stopped pulsing—do you want to cut it?"

"Yes, please."

Handing him the surgical scissors, she clamped close to the baby's belly and showed him where to cut. It was sliced through in a second and looked perfect. Just like the newborn.

A half hour later the baby was snug and safe, and Carly had completed the documents that recorded the birth and cleaned up her instruments.

"I'm going to go so you can get acquainted with your little one." The couple's other two children had slept through the birth, so they wouldn't meet their new sister until tomorrow.

Gloria reached for her, gripping her hand. "Thank you so much for coming. We couldn't have done it without you."

"I loved being here. I'm glad everything went so well." She smiled at the baby, who was already nursing. "I'll see myself out. Call me if you have any questions or concerns."

"We will. Thank you again."

Carly left the house and climbed into her car. Now that the rush of adrenaline had worn off, she was flat tired. Exhausted, in fact.

She drove to the first traffic light, only to have it turn red just before she arrived. All she wanted was to get home and climb in bed. She was due at the clinic in three short hours. If it weren't for Adem, she would have called to see if someone could cover for her for a couple of hours, but the sonogram machines were due to arrive this morning, and she really didn't want him to know she'd been out this late at night. Although that was ridiculous. He was just as apt to get a middle-of-the-night call from the hospital asking him to come look at a head trauma.

Resting her hands on the top of the steering wheel, she waited for the light. When it turned green she started through the intersection. From the corner of her eye she saw a movement and slammed on her brakes, but not soon enough to avoid the vehicle that hit full force against the side of her car. She felt herself spinning, head whipping around to the side, her foot still pressed hard against the brake. Her hand went to her stomach as she finally came to a jerking stop. She sat there for what seemed like an eternity, feeling a warm trickle down the side of her right temple.

She reached over to unbuckle the seat belt and then realized with horror that she hadn't pushed the bottom section down her hips as far as she should have, and that in keeping her from crashing through her windshield, her body had lunged against the belt with terrific force.

A sense of nausea built in her chest, and she leaned sideways, vomiting onto the seat. The street was eerily silent and there was no sound from anyone in the other car. Were they hurt? Wiping the back of her hand across her mouth, she reached over to try to find her cell phone, thankfully locating it immediately.

Oh, God, her baby. How hard had she hit that seat belt? Hard enough that her chest hurt from the impact.

She glanced at the screen and saw her last call was from Adem, telling her about the sonogram machines arriving tomorrow. Without thinking, she pushed the button and listened to two rings before her muddled head realized she should be calling emergency services, not Adem. She hung up and dialed the number that everyone knew by heart. In a shaky voice she told them her location and that there was another vehicle, but it was somewhere behind her and she couldn't see…

"Stay in your vehicle. Help is en route."

She lifted her hand to her head to find the source of the bleeding. Something on her temple stung. Maybe she'd hit her head.

The phone buzzed again, and thinking it was the dispatcher calling back she answered, only to hear a sleepy masculine voice. "Carly? Did you try to call me?"

"I… I…" Hearing his voice suddenly made a wall of emotion erupt, and she gave a half-sob.

"Where are you?" His voice sharpened as if he'd suddenly come fully awake.

"At an intersection." She tried to find a sign, but her eyes hurt. "I don't know which one. I had a delivery tonight. A baby girl, like ours." No, wait. She didn't know if it was a girl.

A sense of sleep was starting to take over again, only this didn't quite feel like the normal tiredness she'd had earlier.

"Carly!" His voice made her blink.

"...was an accident. I think...an ambulance."

"Where was your patient? Give me the address."

"Mmm...just want to sleep."

"No! Tell me where you are."

She tried to open her mouth to tell him, but nothing came out. Then doing what she'd longed to do ever since she left Gloria and Ned's house, she laid her head back against the seat, closing her eyes. She still heard Adem's voice off in the distance, but it was growing fainter and fainter as her hand dropped to the seat beside her.

With a sigh, her pain melted away along with her fear and she gave in to the wave that was closing over her head.

Derya Ann. Sleep well, baby.

CHAPTER EIGHT

ADEM SKIDDED INTO the Queen Victoria and practically sprinted past the admissions desk in the A&E, ignoring the shocked eyes of the staff members, some of whom knew him. All he knew was that Carly had been in a car accident, the other driver getting off with barely a scratch, although he was flaming drunk. The man had run a traffic light.

Dammit.

Of course Adem wasn't on Carly's list of emergency contacts, so he was going in there as a doctor and not as the father of her child. He was told she'd hit her head, bringing back eerie memories of the child he'd fought so hard to save but had ultimately lost.

At four in the morning, the hospital

was quieter than during normal operating hours, so at the first shut exam room door, he knocked and then peeked in. There she was. Dane Hampton, one of the other neurosurgeons, was with her.

"How is she?"

The man's head tilted when he saw him. "Adem? I didn't know you were on duty tonight."

And here came the explanations, none of which he had. "It's complicated. She works at the clinic. How is she?"

"I think she may have a slight concussion. We were about to take her to X-ray and make sure nothing else is broken."

"She's pregnant." The words came out before he could stop them. But since Carly hadn't shared the news with anyone other than her mother, he wanted to make sure they knew that before doing radiographs.

Dane glanced at a computer screen. "I see no record of that. Are you sure?"

"Yes. Like I said, she works at the clinic." He swallowed hard. "She told me."

"Confirmed? Or suspected?"

Actually, Adem didn't know if she'd had another pregnancy test done, or if she'd stopped at the one. "She's pretty sure."

"Okay. How far along, do you know?"

"Not far." Let's see, today would make almost four weeks.

Dane made a sound in his throat. "She's got bruising from the seat belt on her chest and across her abdomen."

Her abdomen?

He swore. Was the baby okay? Hell, none of that mattered right now. All he was concerned about was Carly.

"Has she regained consciousness?"

"Not yet. I pulled her records. She was out on a call, had just left the location."

At four in the morning? No, the call would have come earlier. But she had to be exhausted.

"Any sign of anything else going on?"

"Her pupils are normal and reactive. Blood pressure and temp are normal. As far as I can tell, she just conked her head."

Almost as soon as he said it, Carly's eyes fluttered and then opened, trailing around the room. He went up to the bed and looked down at her, ignoring the need to take her hand. "Hey. How are you feeling?"

"The baby?"

"I'm sure the baby is fine." The last thing he wanted to do was scare her.

"Hmm..." Her eyes closed for a second before reopening. "We still haven't thought of a boy's name yet."

Dane's glance sharpened, coming to rest on him. He nodded toward the back of the room. When Adem followed him, he said, "Is there something I should know?"

It wasn't up to him to tell the other doctor anything. That was Carly's decision.

"Like I said, it's complicated. I just want to make sure she's okay." He would figure out all of the other stuff later. No need to tell the other man that they'd slept together but were not in a relationship, even though he knew Dane wasn't a gossip.

"That's what I'm trying to do. But if you

have any personal involvement with this… *patient*…then you need to take a step back and let me handle this."

Dane was right. He knew he was. But man, turning Carly over to him was not an easy pill to swallow. "I know."

"Let me finish examining her, and then I'll come out and let you know. But thanks for telling me about the pregnancy. I've called her mother. She's on her way in."

Great. So much for setting up a time to meet her. It looked like fate had taken that out of both of their hands.

"Thanks." He hesitated. "If you could keep this between us for now, I would appreciate it."

"As long as Carly doesn't tell me something untoward happened between you, then what happens between staff members is their business, not mine. I met my wife at this hospital." He said it with a smile.

Little did the man know that he and Carly weren't getting married. Or engaged. Nor anything that remotely looked like the joining of two lives.

Hadn't that already happened, though?

"I'll be in my office."

"Okay, I'll see about having her ultrasounded. If she's three or four weeks out, we should be able to see the gestational sac at least. But we probably won't know the effect on the pregnancy for at least a couple of days. If she miscarries, it'll be somewhere in that time frame."

Trudging to his office was hard. But he couldn't demand to be there with her. He'd already closed the door on anything that smacked of commitment.

How about saying he wanted to be a part of the baby's life? Didn't that constitute commitment?

Not in the eyes of the hospital or the law. Carly was the only one who could give permission for him to know anything.

And that sucked. Big-time.

Once she was well enough, he was going to ask to be included on her emergency contact list. If she hadn't called him, he wouldn't have even known she was in an accident until after he arrived at work and realized she was missing. He didn't like that.

What if she'd been killed?

Or her brain had started swelling?

He closed his eyes, pinching the bridge of his nose between his fingers to stop the tension headache that was gathering.

And if she didn't want him on that list? He really had no right to demand to be notified, even though the baby was his.

It wasn't just the baby. He genuinely cared what happened to her.

Dammit. If he wanted to meet her mother, maybe he should go to the waiting room instead of hiding out in his office. With that thought in mind, he started to get up from his chair, only to have his mobile ring.

Thank God.

He answered. "Carly. Are you okay? The baby?"

A female voice who was definitely not

Carly answered. "This is Madelaine Eliston, Carly's mom. She asked me to call you. Are you…?"

The voice trailed away. "Her baby's father? Yes."

"I see. She talked about wanting to introduce us. Can we meet?"

This wasn't exactly how he'd imagined this going down. Hell, he'd tried not to imagine it at all, but here it was. It made him realize that he probably wasn't going to be able to keep this from his parents for long, and that the idea of trying wasn't a good thing. Carly was handling all of this much better than he was.

"Is she still being examined?"

"Yes, they're doing an ultrasound right now. I'm in the waiting room. Do you want to come here?"

He certainly didn't want her coming to his office. Not after what had happened in here. "Yes, I'll be right down."

Heading down the lift back to the ground floor, he made his way to the spot where

Carly's mom was waiting for him. He definitely wasn't skidding down any halls like he had half an hour earlier. Really, all he wanted to do right now was find out how Carly was. Whether the ultrasound showed anything they could make any sense out of.

He recognized her right away. With red hair and a calm demeanor, she looked very much like her daughter. "Mrs. Eliston?"

"You're Mr. Kepler?"

"Yes, but call me Adem, please."

"I want you to know that I'm very happy for Carly. And she's thrilled."

"Thank you. I'm pretty happy as well."

He was. The accident had focused his thoughts, helped him put his priorities in order.

And if it were too late?

Hell, everything had to be okay. To lose the baby now…

He decided to ask. "Have you heard anything more?"

"Carly has a wicked headache, but the other doctor told me that's pretty normal with a concussion. I can't believe a drunk driver hit her. When will people learn?"

"Unfortunately not soon enough."

A doctor was headed their way, but it wasn't Dane this time. It was the same obstetrician that had consulted with him on Naomi's case. Raphael Dubois.

He glanced at Adem and then at Madelaine. "Are you Carly's mother?"

"I am."

He frowned slightly. "I thought Dane was doing her neurological workup."

"He is. I'm here as a friend of the family." He didn't know what else to say, and the slight tightening of Madelaine's mouth said she wasn't sure she liked the title he'd given himself. But it was too late now.

"Well, we did the ultrasound, and there is definitely a gestational sac there. We're hoping the trauma from the seat belt hasn't shaken things up too much and that the baby stays put. I take it she wants to continue with the pregnancy?"

"Yes." Madelaine said the word before

he could get it out, and a good thing because Raphael might start wondering how Adem—a "friend of the family"—would know that Carly wanted her pregnancy to continue.

"Okay, good. Mr. Hampton would like her admitted for observation until tomorrow. Then she needs about a week off to make sure there are no ill effects from the concussion. Are you okay with that? Can Carly come and stay with you for a couple of days?"

That thought suddenly didn't sit well with him. He wasn't sure why, other than he wanted Carly home with him. Where he could keep an eye on her and the baby.

"Yes, of course."

"Great. As soon as we get her settled in a room, you can both go in and see her."

"Thank you."

Left alone once again, Madelaine smiled at him. "She said you're a very nice man, and I believe that."

Did she? Well, Adem wasn't too sure of

that right now. "Thanks. She's a wonderful woman."

"Yes, she is. I don't know how all of this came about, but she believes you want what's best for the baby."

"I do, without a doubt."

"That's good to know. Do you also want what's best for Carly? Someone once walked out on her at a very difficult time in her life. I don't want to see her hurt like that again."

By the fiancé she'd told him about? He thought he wanted what was best for all of them. But did he really? Or was he more concerned with his own comfort and trying to change his life as little as possible?

If that was true, then he would not be as good a man as Carly believed. But he had no idea how he should view her. As someone he'd shared a few passionate hours with? Or something more?

Damn. He didn't know. All he knew was that she had somehow got under his skin in a way that no one else had. And it worried him. Made him wonder if all of his plans for his life were about to implode in his face. All of those lectures to himself about not becoming like his dad…

Madelaine was still waiting for an answer to her question. "I'd like to think I want what's best for her. I care about her."

That much was true. Would always be true.

She studied his face for several long seconds before saying, "That's all I needed to hear. Thank you." She then came over and gave him a quick hug, which made him wince.

She probably shouldn't thank him quite yet. He was still very capable of doing something that would hurt Carly, even unintentionally. But he was starting to think more and more that maybe he shouldn't have been so quick to dismiss the idea of marriage. Instead, he'd given a knee-jerk response that he might come to regret.

A nurse came over. "You can see Carly

now. It looks like she might have quite a shiner by morning."

She was going to have a black eye? His chest tightened as he thought of how lucky she was that that was all she would have. She could have been killed. Or received a traumatic injury from which she might never recover.

She could still lose the baby.

No. He was not going to think along those lines. Especially knowing what he did about the removal of her ovary and the possibility that she might not be able to get pregnant again, if something happened to the second one.

"I'll let you go in first," he said to Madelaine.

"I think we should both go in. So that she knows we've met and that we're not at each other's throats."

"Did you think we would be?"

"*I* didn't." She laughed. "But Carly gave me a stiff warning, telling me to be nice."

Madelaine had the air of someone who

was almost always nice. But he'd bet like any parent she could come down hard on someone who brought harm to their child. Wasn't that why she'd asked him if he had Carly's best interests at heart?

Of course it was. It was probably not so much a question as a reminder.

"Well, she'll be happy to know that you've been a lot nicer than you should have been."

She smiled again, and he found more hints of her daughter in her facial expressions. "I don't think I have. Carly seems happy about what's happened, and that's enough for me. She respects you a lot. Even before any of this happened. She said you were doing good work in the community. And she was very excited about the ultrasound machines."

She'd talked to her mum about him? No two families could have been more different. He very rarely shared any information about his work life with his folks. Nor did they ask. His dad didn't, anyway, other than to ask if he was doing okay for himself.

"I'm happy about those machines as well. I think it'll make the clinic even more self-sufficient."

"Carly thinks so too." She motioned toward the hallway. "Shall we go see her?"

Carly looked past her aching head to see her mother and Adem coming into the room.

"Hi." She was a little nervous that they were here together. This wasn't quite the way she'd envisioned doing these introductions. Especially since her brain seemed a little sluggish right now.

Her mom came over and kissed her cheek. "We were both worried."

"I was a little worried myself." Her voice seemed to come from a distance as she tried to focus.

Adem hadn't said anything yet, and she licked her lips. They hadn't been able to tell her with any certainty that the pregnancy would remain viable. And if she miscarried?

Well, he would have no reason to stick

around. No reason to go on boating trips or sit in the park with her. And she found that bothered her. Very, very much. She just wasn't sure why, although her head was busy trying to work something out.

There was no way to know how he would react, unless it happened. And God, she did not want to lose this baby. Not after everything that had happened.

Derya Ann, please still be in there.

She was going to be devastated if she lost it to something so very stupid like a car accident. If she'd just looked a third time before starting across that intersection…

"The other driver. Was he hurt?"

Her mother made a scoffing sound. "Not a bit. It doesn't seem fair, does it? He was drunk and ran a red light, and then gets to walk away without a scratch."

"I'm glad he's okay."

Her mom gripped her hand. "So, the doctor says you have a concussion, but that you should be fine."

"I know. He came in and talked to me.

I'm surprised my hard head couldn't take a little tap like that."

"It was more than a little tap, sweetheart. Your car is totaled."

Adem still hadn't said anything, and she was getting even more nervous. Maybe it was because her mom was here. She could be a little intimidating when she wanted to. That came part and parcel with being a single mom and having to make all the decisions herself. Some of that had rubbed off on Carly as well.

Had she said something to Adem that he hadn't liked?

She'd warned her to be nice to him. And honestly, Adem wasn't a hothouse flower. He was very capable of standing up for himself.

She couldn't stand it any longer. She was going to make him say something. "Adem, when did you get here?"

He slowly walked toward the bed. "You hung up on me after saying you'd been in an accident, so I had no idea where you were. The only thing I could think of doing was coming here."

There was something strained in his voice. A tiny thread of what she'd heard on the night when his patient had taken a turn for the worse. He was worried.

About the baby?

Well, she'd been worried too.

But it wasn't just that. What she saw in his face was different.

"Hey. I'm okay." The urge to hold her hand out for him to take swept over her, but with her mom standing right there, she didn't think he would appreciate it.

As if reading her mind, her mom leaned down and kissed her on the cheek. "I'll let you guys talk for a few minutes while I see if I can find some decent coffee in this place."

Carly smiled. "I'm glad you came."

"You're my world, sweetheart. I wouldn't want to be anywhere else."

"I know." Her mom loved her more than

she could possibly deserve. She would do anything for them.

"I'll be back in about fifteen minutes."

She guessed that was her mom's way of warning her to do whatever talking they had to do in that time frame. Or maybe she was worried about coming in and finding them kissing. Or worse.

Not much chance of that with the way she was feeling. Her head really did hurt.

But probably not as bad as Naomi's had.

Her mom was out the door and Carly turned her attention back to Adem, trying to find a smile. "I never did get to try that Turkish coffee you promised me."

He didn't say anything nor did he smile, and as the seconds stretched toward minutes, she began to worry.

"You didn't tell me where you were." Those were the first real words out of his mouth.

"I'm sorry, Adem. I was confused. I'd been thinking about other things on the drive home and was on autopilot. It was late, and I was already sleepy, so I think that combined with the accident just knocked me for a loop."

He did what she'd wanted to do: threaded his fingers through hers. "Are you really okay?"

"I am. I just want the baby to be okay as well. If something happens to her…"

This time he did smile, and it lit up her world. "So you're doing it as well."

"Doing what as well?"

"Thinking of the baby as a she."

She giggled, then put a hand to her head. "Ugh. Laughing hurts. But yes. I'm already thinking of her as Derya Ann. We really do need to come up with a boy's name at some point, just so they both have equal time."

"We could always change Derya to Derrin, if the baby turns out to be a boy."

"I don't like Derrin. At all."

He squeezed her hand. "Okay. No Derrin. Dexter?"

"No."

"Let's talk about that later." He went and

grabbed a chair that was folded against the wall and pulled it up to the bed. "You were on a call?"

She stiffened. "Yes. It's my job."

"I wasn't criticizing you. I know how much your patients mean to you. I just want to make sure that you call those in so they can get added to the log. What if you'd been knocked unconscious and hadn't been able to call anyone? It would help me know where to look."

It would help *him* know where to look?

That simple sentence struck a chord in her. He really had been worried. About her, and not just the baby.

"Yes, Mr. Administrator, I logged the call. I also called Emergency Services, so they also knew where to look. And my car is even equipped with that nifty little voice response system that I can use to call for help and has a tracker on it. It wasn't very likely that I would have lain in the middle of the street for very long. Someone would have come across the accident and called it in."

"Okay, I'll give you that." He paused. "I want to ask you something."

"Go ahead."

"Your mother asked if I had your best interests at heart."

She licked her lips. "She's my mom, she has to ask questions like that."

"Well, she's right. If you ever feel I don't, I would like you to tell me."

"Yeah, I'm not going to do that. No one knows my best interests but me. I'm like my mom that way. I've learned to look out for myself and tend to value my independence. So even if you think you know…maybe you don't… Or wait." She shook her head. "Ask me that again when my head doesn't feel like it's been stuffed with cotton."

"Sorry. You're right. We'll save that for later. How about this? Mr. Hampton thinks you should stay at someone's house for a week. He was looking at your mum when he said it, but what do you think about… coming home with me?"

"What? No, that would be a terrible idea."

He let go of her hand, and she realized her head injury really was affecting her. "I mean, it would be terrible because we've seen what happens when I come to your apartment. 'Tours' tend to happen. Tours that result in…" She rubbed her hand on her belly, wincing when she hit a sore spot.

"Are you okay?"

"Mmm…yes, it's just where the seat belt caught me." She swallowed, remembering something. "I should have put it lower on my abdomen, but I was tired and wanted to get home. I won't make that mistake again."

"Okay, so no coming to live with me… unless…" He hesitated. "Would you live with me if we were married?"

"But we're not."

He leaned forward, eyes fastened to hers. "Carly, we could be."

There was a strange intensity in his voice that pulled at something deep inside of her.

A kernel of longing that horrified her. He didn't love her. This was about the baby. Nothing more. Nothing less. Like she'd told him a few minutes ago, no one knew her best interests but her. And after her broken engagement, she'd become an expert at self-preservation. And that warning light had just switched itself on.

She swallowed. "No. We couldn't."

"We get along well, we work well together." He attempted a smile. "We agree on a girl's name."

Could he hear himself right now? He sounded like what he'd said about his parents...about their reasons for getting married. That it had been for every reason except the right one: love.

There was no way. She wanted no part of that. Despite her achy head, it was the one thing she knew.

So she said very, very clearly, "No, Adem. I do not want to marry you. Not now. Not ever."

Carly's chest suddenly felt crammed full

of the coils he'd put in Naomi's head, and they were slowly cutting off the blood supply to her heart. She was never marrying anyone for reasons other than love. And not just any love. It had to be the kind that flowed in both directions. It was the only way to remain viable, just like the baby nestled in her womb needed a two-way exchange of nutrients. One without the other… Well, that never ended well. She couldn't live without that.

Not even for Adem.

Her mom swept into the room just as he opened his mouth to say something more. Carly was glad. Glad she wasn't going to have to listen to him present her with yet another argument. One that might sound logical to everyone except for her. Besides, it wouldn't matter. Nothing was going to change her mind.

Nothing.

She smiled as her mom talked about what her orchestra would be playing at the next concert a few weeks from now and how she'd love for Adem to come and hear them. But Carly didn't care about concerts. Or anything else. What she did care about was the bleak look that had suddenly appeared in Adem's eyes. A look she didn't understand, but that filled her with foreboding.

He should be rejoicing that he'd dodged that particular bullet yet again, but he didn't look that way. He looked almost…lost.

No, that wasn't right. It had to be her concussion interfering with her thoughts again. The man didn't love her. He'd told her once that he didn't even believe love existed, or something to that effect. So what had brought that offer on?

His brother and his wife? His parents?

No, she had a feeling it was because he wanted to keep an eye on her…make sure nothing else happened that would possibly endanger his baby.

No. Not his baby. *Their* baby.

She had to make sure she kept emphasizing that point, so he didn't start thinking he could make decisions she disagreed with. Like marrying him.

Although he'd suggested, not insisted.

Was there a difference?

She was pretty sure there was.

But she couldn't ask him, because he was getting up, smiling a smile that looked as fake as all get-out. "I have an appointment this morning that I need to go to. But I'll check in on you later. Call me if you need me."

"Okay." She wasn't going to call him for anything. But she wouldn't say that in front of her mom, who would read way more into the words than she should. "See you later. Thanks for checking on me."

"Not a problem."

Except she felt like it was. Only she had no idea what that problem was. Or why. But now wasn't the time to ask him. She could do that later, when he did come to check on her.

Except Adem didn't come later. Nor did he call to see how she was doing. She chalked it up to his being busy and went home the next day with her mom, just like they'd planned. There would be plenty of time to talk later. They could then hammer out what they'd talked about, even if last night was kind of a blur. One thing she did remember, though, was that Adem had asked her to marry him. And she'd been fixated on two-way flows and why marriage between them could never work, because that love would only flow in one direction. From her. To him.

Her mind seized, grabbing that thought and tearing it apart until a stunning realization overtook her.

She loved the man. Had probably loved him from the time she'd asked him to leave the restaurant with her. She just hadn't recognized it for what it was.

And so his proposal should have made her heart sing, should make her want to jump up and shout it from the rooftops, but it hadn't.

Because it had come from a place of duty.

Of following in the path that his parents had paved.

In the end she'd turned him down. Not because she wanted to. But because his offer of marriage had seemed to come for all the wrong reasons.

But what if it hadn't? What if his reasons hadn't been wrong at all?

Maybe she needed to sit down and think about what it all meant. To put some kind of brakes on a train that had been running away for far too long. And she knew exactly where she could start.

CHAPTER NINE

SHE'D TURNED HIM DOWN.

Adem sat in his office at the clinic, two portable ultrasound machines at the ready. The tech was coming to demonstrate them this afternoon, and Carly wouldn't be here for it. She was still at her mum's house, would be for another couple of days. He'd decided not to call her, since he'd got the rundown on her condition from Raphael. As far as they knew the pregnancy was still viable, and since she hadn't contacted him either, maybe it was true.

Maybe the woman was just so horrified by what he'd asked that she couldn't bring herself to look at him. After all, what was it that she'd said?

I do not want to marry you. Not now. Not ever.

She'd seen right through his request, and she'd been right to turn him down. So very right.

The words had just appeared on his tongue out of nowhere and out they'd come. She'd once told him she wouldn't settle for anything other than love. And he'd once told her he'd never felt that particular emotion, wasn't sure if he even believed in it.

So how was it that he was sitting here, wondering why he felt like he'd been run over by a truck and left for dead?

Maybe because the one emotion he'd never believed in—never thought he was capable of feeling—had reached around and grabbed him by the throat. It couldn't be real. It had to be something to do with the baby.

Except he couldn't for the life of him figure out how he could mix up the two. When Carly was in that accident he'd panicked when her voice had begun fading away, and it had had nothing to do with the baby. That worry had been all about Carly.

Maybe that had been part of the tragedy of his parents. Maybe one of them had learned to love and one of them hadn't. How torturous of a union would that be to love someone and never have it returned?

It wouldn't be fair to him and it definitely wouldn't be fair to Carly. He was not condemning her to that kind of existence, even if she had agreed to his crazy proposition.

So what did he do about it? How did they work together and not either come to resent being thrown together time and time again or fall back into the pattern of sleeping together, knowing it was going no further than that?

Carly's mom had asked him if he had her best interests at heart.

His phone rang and he glanced to see it was his brother. Damn. He did not want to talk to Basir right now. But it might be important.

Answering the call, he leaned back in his office chair, staring at the new machines. "Hello?"

"Adem, what the hell is going on?"

He'd never heard Basir raise his voice. Ever. But right now there was an anger in his tone that was impossible to mistake. "What are you talking about?"

"Our midwife is leaving."

He sat forward in a rush. "She what?"

"I just got off the phone with her. She said she'd decided to transfer out of the clinic to the Queen Victoria and that she was notifying her patients that she'd only be available to those who would be having their babies there."

Carly loved being a community midwife. She'd told him that time and time again, had told him how much good the Victoria Clinic was doing in the surrounding neighborhoods. So what on earth would possess her to…

He had. He and his stupid proposal. Hadn't he just been sitting here thinking about how hard it was going to be to keep working together?

Evidently Carly had decided it wasn't just hard…it was impossible.

So she was quitting?

"Honestly, Basir, this is the first I've heard about it. Carly was in an accident a few days ago and was pretty shaken up. I'll talk to her and see—"

"She also said she was pregnant and that our due dates were going to be a little over a month apart."

And it was time to confess. At least to his brother. "The baby is mine."

"Excuse me?"

"I'm the father of Carly's baby."

"But—"

"Exactly. We haven't told anyone, and maybe that has something to do with all of this. I asked her to marry me, and she turned me down."

"Why would she do that?"

"I wasn't sure at the time. But I think I'm coming to understand her reasons."

"Wow, Adem. I had no idea." There was a pause. "Do you love her?"

At least there was one member of their family who understood what was truly important.

No, make that two. Because his brother had just hit the nail on the head. He loved the woman.

"Hell. I think I do. But I'm pretty sure I've screwed everything up." He dragged a hand through his hair. "I'll talk to her, but I can't make any promises."

"Then don't. Just talk to her." There was a pause. "Let's make this generation of Keplers different from the last and learn to lead with our hearts."

"I don't know if I can do that."

"Yes. You can. You just don't know if you will."

With that, Basir hung up the phone, leaving Adem staring off into the distance.

His brother was right. He could. But he wasn't sure if he would. Or if he should. But what he could do was take away Carly's reasons for leaving the clinic by doing something he'd mentioned to her right after she'd discovered she was pregnant. She'd been vehemently opposed at the time, but now she might find herself relieved. Hadn't he said that no one person was irreplaceable?

So he was faced with one of the hardest decisions he'd ever made. Do what was in Carly's best interest. Or his own.

The answer to that seemed pretty damned simple and yet so damned hard. But what choice did he have?

None, if he wanted to do the right thing.

Taking a deep breath, he picked up the phone and dialed her number.

Carly listened to the voice mail for the third time, unable to believe her ears. Adem was going to resign?

Basir had to have told him about their phone conversation. She should have called Adem first, but she hadn't wanted him to try to talk her out of transferring to the hospital.

But to say he was going to quit so that she didn't have to?

God. She should have answered that call. But she'd been a mess. And now, unfortunately, he'd beaten her to the punch. She hadn't yet turned her paperwork in for the transfer; she'd wanted to notify her patients first. Maybe she'd been putting off the inevitable for as long as possible. But if she did it now, then they might both wind up at the hospital, working together all over again, in a huge dose of irony.

Her head was completely better, no residual headache, and her pregnancy was still going strong, thank God. Both were things to rejoice over. She hadn't seen Adem, but after the way they'd left things, she wasn't surprised that he hadn't tried to call her. Until now.

He'd probably felt as awkward as she did. But now that she was well enough to contemplate going into his office and setting things straight—to put them back the way they'd been before the accident—she found she might be too late.

He said he was going to make it official at the next hospital board meeting, but that until then he would do as much of his work as possible at his office at the hospital, so she wouldn't have to see him.

Wouldn't have to see him?

Why? Why? Why?

The thought of him being gone forever pecked at her insides, turning them into a war zone, even though she'd been the one who'd originally planned on leaving.

That last sentence of his voice mail had been a joke. *Things at the clinic will continue just like usual.*

No. No, they wouldn't.

A thin stream of anger bubbled up inside of her. He was being ridiculous. Her thoughts whirled back to almost a month ago when she'd first told him about her pregnancy. He'd thought about resigning then, but she thought she'd talked him out of it. And now they were back where they started. All because he'd asked her to marry him.

Love had to flow both ways to be viable.

Hadn't he said he would never get married, that he didn't want to live like his parents did? He wasn't even willing to *pretend.*

He'd had a strange intensity in his voice after the accident when he'd talked about marriage. One that hadn't been there in his earlier discussions.

Her heart picked up the pace. After she'd told him she would never, ever marry him, he acted strangely. She remembered thinking that she would have to talk to him once she was better to figure out how to get them back to the place they were before. And then he'd left the room, saying he would check on her later. But he hadn't. She actually hadn't heard from him again, until that phone call, which she now found odd. More than odd.

He'd been so worried about her when she was fading from consciousness in that car, and then again at the hospital.

And then he'd asked her to marry him.

Carly...we could be.

The way he'd looked at her. The way he'd said it.

Had he really meant it? As something more than what his parents had?

He'd never said love, had never even hinted that that's what was behind the proposal.

But what if it was? What if it really did flow both ways?

She mulled those words over in her mind. She knew he cared about her. Her mom told her that he'd used that exact wording when they'd spoken together in the waiting room.

But what about love?

Her head came up, the emotionless tones from Adem's voice mail forgotten. Why had she been so fervent in her rejection of what he'd asked her.

Because she didn't want to marry if it wasn't for love.

But… What. If. It. Was?

Adem had told her he'd never felt love.

Didn't even believe in the emotion. But what if that had changed?

She loved him. But could he possibly…by some stretch of the imagination…?

Her thoughts whirled back through a hundred different images. Herself with her hands against that glass window. In the park, telling him about the baby, and how his face had changed when he realized he was going to be a father. On the boat laughing over silly baby names. In the hospital as he stood over her, concern and…fear… on his face. The urgency behind his offer of marriage.

That's why his proposal had seemed so horrifying to her. And why she'd ultimately decided to leave the clinic. She'd wanted him to love her. Wanted that marriage proposal to come out of the right place.

Maybe it had.

Maybe that's why he was suddenly so ready to leave the clinic so that she didn't have to. Sacrificing himself for her, in the same way she'd been ready to do for him.

She swallowed hard. Could it be that easy? And that impossibly hard?

So what did she do? Just let things remain like they were? Let Adem leave the clinic for her?

Hell, no.

The man had made her fall in love with him, despite her best attempts at thwarting Cupid's barrage of arrows. The least he could do was stand there and tell her what she meant to him. What *they* meant to him, because she and the baby were kind of a package deal at the moment.

She just had to somehow confront him where he couldn't get up and run away. Or resign. Where he would have to sit and tell her exactly what she did or didn't mean to him.

And she thought she knew the perfect place.

All she had to do was get a little help from a certain brainy cellist, who'd already laid the perfect foundation for what Carly had in mind.

CHAPTER TEN

ADEM DIDN'T KNOW why he was here.

Shepherd Hall was built to impress, with white marble columns and polished steps that led up to the huge venue. It was where countless concerts and musicals took place.

Standing at the base of the stairs with people streaming around him, he hesitated, ticket in hand.

Carly's mom had called him and reissued her invitation—the one she'd given at the hospital—asking him to attend her orchestra's first concert of the season. Had kept him on the phone until he promised to come.

Maybe she didn't know that he would soon be gone from the clinic, or that he and Carly hadn't spoken since that last day at the hospital.

He could have refused to attend. It had been on the tip of his tongue to say he had other plans, but something had made him accept the complimentary ticket. Maybe the faint hope that he would catch a glimpse of Carly somewhere in the crowded theater. She said she always attended her mother's first concert of the season.

Find her among all these people? Not likely.

Damn. He loved her. And the baby. It seemed like that should have solved all of his problems. Instead, it seemed to have compounded them.

Unless he tried again. Unless he sat down with Carly and had a long talk. They'd tried on the boat. And he'd tried at the hospital. But their connections just kept getting crossed.

So why not try to uncross them. He hadn't exactly bared his soul during his ridiculous proposal. Instead, he'd made it sound like something out of his father's playbook instead of his own.

Basir's suggestion that this generation should get off to a fresh start made sense. And was part of the reason he'd agreed to come.

And if Carly really was here somewhere? Well, he would never find her…unless…

Moving out of the line of people surging up the steps, he pulled his phone out of the pocket of his tuxedo and found her in his contact list. Just as he started to dial the number a hand linked through his arm.

He glanced to the side, ready with an apology, when green eyes met his.

"Carly?"

With her red hair piled on top of her head, and dark sultry liner beneath her lashes, she was almost unrecognizable. And that dress…

Damn. It wasn't the navy blue she'd been carrying all those weeks ago at the hospital. This was raven black and devastating to the senses, the gathered bodice hugging her form like a glove, before billowing out into a soft cloud of fabric. She was stunning. Sophisticated. The very picture of the woman he'd imagined didn't exist, once upon a time. A woman who'd shown him just how much fun she could have, taking him on a ride to a distant land. Where things were different from how he'd believed them to be.

"Hello, Adem. I see you have a ticket too."

Was this real? Or had he somehow conjured her up?

"Yes. Compliments of your mother."

A passing thought slid through his head, and he grabbed it. "Do you think she's playing matchmaker?"

"Nope. My mom would never do that." Her fingers tightened on his arm. "But I might."

She sounded like that siren who'd once caused him to abandon his dinner just to hold her in his arms. The siren who'd comforted him when he'd been in a pit of despair.

The siren who now carried his child.

And he hoped to God he understood what she was saying.

"You're playing matchmaker?"

"I am. Interested?"

He cupped her face in his hands and stared down at her. Yes, he saw the playful temptress in there, but he also saw hints of a vulnerable woman trying to find her way through this thing called life.

That was okay. Because right now, he was a vulnerable man, trying to do the same.

"I am interested. More than you can imagine actually. But I have one condition."

She frowned. "What's that?"

"That there are no more games, and that you tell me exactly how you feel about me."

Her frown disappeared, and a slow smile appeared. "That's easy. Very easy. I love you." She wrapped her arms around his waist. "I have a condition of my own."

"Okay..."

"I want you to tear up whatever resignation letter you might be drafting."

"Done. How about if neither one of us leaves the clinic?"

"But I don't want to cause problems if people—"

He silenced her with a kiss. "There are husband and wife doctor teams at hospitals everywhere. Why not a surgeon/midwife team. It seems we worked pretty well together once upon a time." His thumbs stroked her jawline, glorying when he felt her shiver. "And before you say anything, that's not why I asked you to marry me that day in your hospital room. I loved you then. I didn't know it at the time, but I was desperate to get you to say yes. And so I spouted off a reason that seemed rational at the time, but in doing so, I left off the most important reason of all. The only one worth saying yes to: love."

He pressed his forehead to hers, wondering if Carly's mum really had read his thoughts that day at the hospital. "Carolyn Eliston. Will you marry me? For love, this time?"

Carly stood on her tiptoes, pressing her cheek to his. "Yes. Oh yes. But only for love."

The meeting of lips was long and luscious and full of all things good and honest and real. When he pulled back she was breathless and smiling. And damn if she didn't glow.

Well, that was okay, because he was walking on air.

"Shall we go in and watch the orchestra?"

"Yes. And then afterward we can go back to your place."

Adem laughed and then wrapped his arm around her waist as they walked up the steps. "You read my mind. You'll be happy to know that I've revamped my tour program to include several new and exciting stops."

As they found their seats and the sound of the symphony swirled around them in the intimacy of the dark theater, Adem proceeded to whisper them to her, one sexy destination at a time.

EPILOGUE

ADEM TOLD HIS parents the news a few days later as she stood beside him in support, fingers linked together. He'd told her more about his folks' strained relationship, telling her that he wanted his marriage to Carly to be completely different. If anything, it made her love him even more.

His father's forbidding frown gave way to a softer look as he listened as Adem explained how much he loved Carly and how important it was to both of them that they start off their marriage knowing they had each other's support and love.

"So I am to be a grandfather twice? Both you *and* Basir?"

"Yes. Both of us."

Adem's mom glanced at her husband. "Isn't this great news, Selim?"

"Yes. It is."

And the strangest thing happened. Selim's arm slid around his wife's waist, making her eyes widen for a second before she turned back to the front, a slight smile playing at her lips.

Adem leaned down and kissed Carly's temple in a display that was far more open than that of his parents, but from what he'd told her, even something as simple as an arm around a waist was a major departure from what the pair had shared before.

Maybe this was a new start for everyone. Carly hoped so. And whether things changed permanently for Adem's parents or not, all she knew was that she was never going back to the life she'd had before.

Oh, she intended to stay independent, but the moments of loneliness she'd had before were gone. She knew that she and her baby were both loved for who they were.

And Carly intended to take nothing for granted. She was going to enjoy every minute she got to spend with the man she loved.

And she knew that Adem had vowed to do the same. They were getting married. The sooner, the better.

Not because they had to, but because they loved each other.

And that love was enough to carry them through for the rest of their lives.

* * * * *